本书获得中华人民共和国新闻出版总署"经典中国国际出版工程"资助

WU Liangyong: Essays on the Sciences of the Human Settlements in China

Tsinghua University Press

Contents

Sciences of Human Settlements:
Theoretical and
Practical Explorations

1

1.1 The Sciences of Human Settlements in the World

Since C. A. Doxiadis advanced the theory of EKISTICS with the ending of World War Ⅱ, the theory and practice of the Science of Human Settlements has been developed over the world. The UN Habitat Ⅰ Conference in Vancouver in 1976, the RIO Conference in 1992, the UN Habitat Ⅱ Conference in Istanbul in 1996, as well as other worldwide actions up to the UN Special Conference of Istanbul+5 last June, have marked an unceasing progress of the research in this field. The new concepts of Human Settlements, Habitat, cities in the globalizing world, emerging in consequence of the research progress, have become the global guidelines for building a sustainable world. Today, the sustainable development of Human Settlements has become a common theme all over the world and thus architecture and urban planning have been ushered into a broad realm of multidisciplinary cooperation for further development.

Taking into consideration all the current changes, we hereby advocate developing the Sciences of Human Settlements in a more comprehensive way. This means establishing the communities of science, encouraging the collective work and the multidisciplinary communication among all participants, and searching for the theory and approach of a new paradigm.

1.2 Recent Rural and Urban Development in China

It is well known that great changes have taken place in China in the past two decades. These changes can be seen not only in geographical dimensions but also in all socio-economic aspects: politics, economy, culture, science, and technology. Both the economic development and urbanization have stepped into an accelerating phase, leading to a great annual growth of gross domestic product (GDP) and urban population. Amidst magnificent achievements, there have emerged some complicated problems. The crux is that the cities and the countryside are developing at such a rapid rate, on such a large scale, with such enormous capital, to such a vast extent that they have surpassed any historical period that the country has ever witnessed before. Virtually, building construction has today become a major economic pursuit in China.

In the transition from a planned economy to a market economy, China has found out her way in accordance to the specific conditions of the country: the socialist market economy that overemphasizes neither the plan nor the market at the expense of the other. It means that the general plans are still necessary, perhaps even more necessary than before, in the course of this rapid growth. To ensure the sustained development of China in future, we should carry out holistic researches, search for general strategies, and lay out common guidelines. In terms of urbanization, we should in particular study the integrated rural and urban development from the regional viewpoints in the hope that the cities and the countryside would advance side by side and the various regional cultures would coexist.

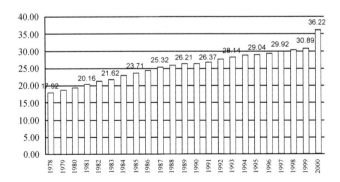

Per Capital GDP in China

by RMB（yuan）

（1USD=8.27yuan RMB in 2000）

Urban Population development in China

Fig. 1.1   Per Capital GDP and Urban Population Development in China

1.3 Theoretical Developments at the Center for Science of Human Settlements of Tsinghua University

Aware of the seriousness of the issues and conscious of the adoption of a scientific approach, I have devoted myself to search for the theory of Science of Human Settlements in China in the past decades with a series of academic publications including "A General Theory of Architecture" in 1989. In 1993, together with my colleagues, I put forward a proposal to set up the Sciences of Human Settlements at the annual conference of Science and Technology Division of the Chinese Academy of Sciences. In order to tackle the problems existing in China's rural and urban construction, we have tried to build a new science focusing on coordination between humans and nature, with the living environment as the major object of study. We have made explorations from various aspects.

Founded in November 1995, the Center for Science of Human Settlements (CSHS) of Tsinghua University has offered a course on "Brief Introduction to Sciences of Human Settlements", and since 1998 offered to publish the "Series on Sciences of Human Settlements" and has made considerable progress in the research field. The steady process marked a good beginning in the field of bright prospects.

Recently, I have published a book entitled "Introduction to Sciences of Human Settlements", which mainly explores the relationship between humans and environments, also with a view of the way out for human settlements in China. The book is divided into two parts. The first part introduces the origins of the Sciences of Human Settlements, its constitutions, its basic ideas, its methodologies, and some case studies that have been carried out by the CSHS in the course of many years' research work on the conservation and development of sustainable human settlements. The second part is on C. A. Doxiadis and Ekistics, which functions as an interpretation and review of the theories of Ekistics. The highlights of the book are summed up in the following sections.

1.3.1 The Connotation of Human Settlements

Human settlement refers to a place where people come to live and build homes.

It functions as the base where people manage to make their life in nature. Man is undoubtedly the core of the settlements. Thus, the primary purpose of building settlements is to meet the demand of humans to live together in communities. According to the density of the residents and the degree of their impact on nature, a human settlement can be divided into two parts in terms of physical space: the ecological environment and the manmade environment. During the long history of evolution of human settlements, the harmonization of man with nature has been always the ideal of mankind, though specific building actions have varied greatly from one another under the influences of natural and social factors.

In detail, human settlement is composed of five systems: nature, man, society, habitation, and network, among which the first two systems are most essential while the last two systems are also indispensable in terms of the construction of physical environment. The relationship between human settlement and its five systems is similar to that between a whole and the parts. Therefore, the achievement of a better human settlement does not lie in the perfection of its systems, but in their integration; and a better human settlement should be not only an ecological environment but also a humanistic one that can meet the demands of mankind, both biological and social individuals.

As a complex system, human settlement involves all kinds of settlements: a room, a village, a town, a city, even the entire world. According to their scale, they can be categorized into five levels: global, regional, city, community, and shell. This categorization is very helpful to clarify some basic concepts in the research of the Sciences of Human Settlements and to set acceptable standards for researches at different levels.

The main purpose of promoting the Sciences of Human Settlements in China today is to try adapting the large-scale constructions to the current circumstances. It suggests that the studies should be carried out not only in the academic field to find out the law of the development but also in the practical field to guide the construction of human settlements that takes place everyday and everywhere. As stated above, a better human settlement, composed of five systems, should be such

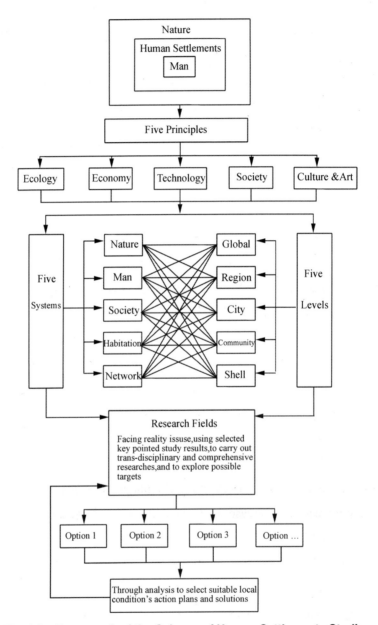

Fig. 1.2 Framework of the Science of Human Settlements Studies

an integration of all its parts that the demands of different aspects would be well satisfied: ecology, economy, science-technology, society, culture-art, etc. From this point of view and with regard to the specific case of China, five principles are proposed herewith as the guidelines for the construction of human settlements: according due respect to nature by promoting ecological awareness of the public and tackling environmental issues; the sound circle between the construction of human settlements and economic development; the prosperity of society promoted by the progress of science and technology; the concerns for the interests of people in terms of individuals as well as society as a whole; and the integration of the pursuit of science and the creation of art.

1.3.2   The Framework of the Sciences of Human Settlements

Taking living environments as the research object, the Sciences of Human Settlements, dealing in a comprehensive way with all the problems occurring during the development of human settlements, is not a mono-discipline but a multi-disciplinary one that involves the sciences of nature, technology, and humanities. It implies that, with the common goal of building an ideal human environment for human beings, all the disciplines concerned with the construction and development of human settlements are regrouped in one framework, centering the trinity of architecture, landscape architecture, and urban planning that work as the leading disciplines.

As the integration of different disciplines, the Sciences of Human Settlements is an adaptive open system that changes ceaselessly. The number of disciplines concerned in the framework may increase or decrease while their importance may also vary from time to time. It should not equate all the disciplines but highlight one or more when it is necessary to deal with practical problems.

The Sciences of Human Settlements advocates a comprehensive, systematic research on human settlements in various aspects. On one hand, the research works could be carried out at any of the five levels of human settlements from the disciplinary perceptions; on the other hand, they could be focused on any of the five systems of human settlements from the regional viewpoints.

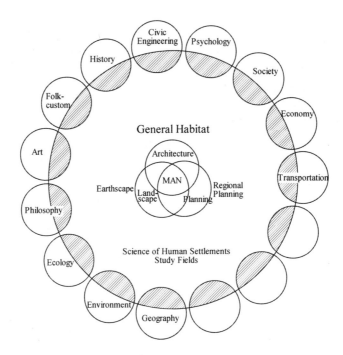

Fig. 1.3 An Open and Creative System for the Sciences of Human Settlements

1.3.3 Research Methodology of the Sciences of Human Settlements

The Sciences of Human Settlements is not an all-powerful discipline that can reach every aspect of human environment. As a complex adaptive system, its feasible method in practice is problem-oriented. First, it aims to identify the key issues from complicated realities, then to channel out the possible solutions to these problems by integrating, in a trans-disciplinary way, the achievements of other concerned disciplines.

From the following figures that we can easy to understand the trans-disciplinary approach was developed. For any researching works, it could be stepped by a single-isolated discipline, or a few disciplines but no linkage; then, a multiple disciplines with some relations; afterward, in a high level cooperation of disciplines intercross; finally, it will be developed into trans-disciplinary with multi-level integration, and trans-discipline process and integrating research steps.

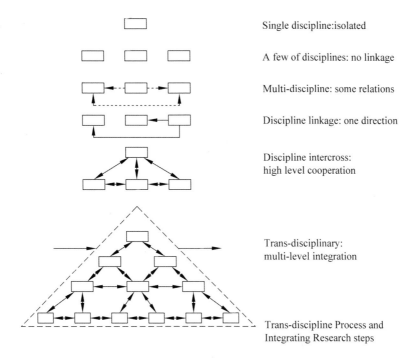

Single discipline:isolated

A few of disciplines: no linkage

Multi-discipline: some relations

Discipline linkage: one direction

Discipline intercross:
high level cooperation

Trans-disciplinary:
multi-level integration

Trans-discipline Process and
Integrating Research steps

Fig. 1.4   From Single Discipline to Trans-disciplinary Integrating Research

Source: Jantsch, Erich. "Inter- and transdisciplinary university: a systems approach to education and innovation". Ekistics, Dec. 1971, vol. 32:193, pp. 430-437

1.3.4   The Theoretical Guidelines for to the Development of Sciences of Human Settlements in China

The Sciences of Human Settlements is a strategic research significant for the development of economy, society, science, and technology of a country. Thus, it is always important to put forward a research schedule that is realistically appropriate. Based on the sustained studies of human settlements in China, I have preliminarily summed up, in my new publication "Introduction to Sciences of Human Settlements", the basic issues for our research of Sciences of Human Settlements under the current circumstances. They concern the coordinative organization of the different disciplines within the framework of the Sciences of Human Settlements, the multi-disciplinary communication and integration of the concerned disciplines, the realistic goals of the development of the Sciences of Human Settlements, and the practical application of the theories and methodologies of the Sciences of Human Settlements in the fields of research, planning, design, and education concerning the construction of human settlements.

• The Guide for Methodology. Just as the Sciences of Human Settlements, composed of different disciplines, is a complex open system that could be approached by a problem-oriented method, Human Settlement, a multi-leveled structure, should be regarded and approached in the same way. Especially in China, the biggest developing country of the world that is now in the accelerating phase of development, the problem of human settlements can only be dealt with as a huge, complex, open system. Thus, researchers working on the Sciences of Human Settlements are required to have a scientific philosophical thinking, a comprehensive understanding of the science of system and the science of complexity, and are required to well master the trans-disciplinary and problem-oriented method to tackle step by step the complicated practical problems. Meanwhile, a community of science should be established, composed of scientists of different disciplines devoted to sustained research for new paradigms.

• The Guide for the Practice of Planning and Design. A holistic thinking is indispensable in the different phases and at the different levels of planning and design. The new theories of planning and design can only be worked out by integrating the various existing ones. Exactly speaking, at the level of architectural design, the theory of General Architecture should be encouraged to enable the return of architectural creations to the basics. At the level of urban design, the new concept of human settlements would lead to the harmony of physical spaces by respecting the perceptions of region, city, community, and building. At the level of general planning and design of human settlements, a new dynamic notion of time and space should be set up to reach the harmonization of time, space, and human beings.

• The Guide for Professional Education. The architectural, landscape, and planning education should be reformed and adapted to the new context to provide the society with new type of qualified persons who are capable of carrying out trans-disciplinary research works and integrating science, humanity, and art. In this view, the training for "professional leadership" and the popularization of the Sciences of Human Settlements would be the key points in future education.

1.4 Practical Developments at the Center for Science of Human Settlements of Tsinghua University

Concerning the advocacy of the Sciences of Human Settlements in China, a considerable number of studies has been done by Tsinghua University in the past half-century, especially in the past 20 years after the economic and political reforms of China. The problem-oriented analysis, the historical and regional study, and the multidisciplinary reference have served as the main methods for the CSHS.

Holistic thinking is the philosophy of the CSHS's planning and design practices. It means that when dealing with a specific project, we always approach it as a part of the whole, as a period in the time sequence, and as an element in a spatial system. The solution is the result of the integration of the past and the future, the element and the entity, the personality, and the harmony.

With accordance to our experiences in the research of Sciences of Human Settlements, the following factors are indispensable for the success:

- The establishment of innovative and industrious academic groups;
- The spirit of cooperation and practical and realistic attitude of the participants;
- The advance of common academic guidelines, academic theories, developmental stratagems, and working methods;
- The organization of research groups, directed by high-level academic leaders, which is made up of the combination of the old, the middle-aged, and the young;
- The promotion of practical problems, which are urgent to be tackled.

1.4.1　Regional Studies

- Sustainable Development of Human Settlements in the Northwest Area of the Yunnan Province. This is a collaborative research between the provincial government of Yunnan and the Tsinghua University, which involved School of Architecture of Tsinghua University and several local institutes of the Yunnan Province. The Northwest Area of Yunnan is distinguished by its richness of ecological and cultural diversities, while suffering from the fragility of environment and backward economic development. Aiming at improving the living environment of the local people, we searched for the potential to accelerate the pace of local economic development, to better preserve the regional feature of ecological and cultural diversities. Some constructive propositions were made: 1) to coordinate the ecological preservation with the socio-economic development by setting up a regional network for preservation of ecological diversity; 2) to encourage the development of tourism and concerned service industries as the key to promoting the local economy; 3) to consciously conserve the diversity of regional cultures under the press of economic growth; 4) to ameliorate the planning, construction, and governance of the living environment. Completed in 1999, the research achieved such a success that all the propositions were accepted by the local government and some of them were even implemented.

• Spatial Development of the Region of Greater Beijing. As one of the most important regional studies in China, this research work was done during the past two years, involving more than 10 research institutes of different cities and hundreds of specialists of different disciplines. It is a successful experiment of the Sciences of Human Settlements in the practical field with the application of problem-oriented methods, trans-disciplinary communication, the collective work of Community of Science, holistic thinking, the Science of Complexity, etc. The research object concerns the territory of the Municipalities of Beijing and Tianjin and the northern part of the Hebei Province. With reference to the experiences of other countries, we approached the region from a global point of view in the following aspects: strategic role, regional function, spatial layout, and mechanism of coordination and cooperation. Based on in-depth analysis of the current situation of the region, the spatial development of Greater Beijing was restructured, aiming at the emergence of a prosperous world city. 1) Combination of organic disposal and rational regroupment in regional dimension. This means to gradually relocate certain urban functions of core cities like Beijing and Tianjin to other cities and to greatly encourage the growth of middle-sized cities to transform Greater Beijing from a mono-centered region to a multi-centered city-region. 2) Macro-control over the actions of land use from the regional level. Forests, agricultural lands, and ecological areas are defined as preservation area or non-development area while the comprehensive remanagement of the valleys is considered an important step to ameliorate the regional environment. 3) Regional cooperation in terms of the construction of a multi-level and multi-functional transportation network. The radio-concentrated pattern should be transformed to a densified network centering two cores with Tianjin being treated as another hub of regional, national, and international communication besides Beijing. 4) Prototype of Transportation Corridor + Urban Cluster + Ecological Network. It is suggested that new urban growth should be reorganized in urban clusters of reasonable size, interrupted by ecological green lands, along several transportation corridors. 5) Enhancement of regional governance and establishment of cooperative and coordinative mechanism. Regional organizations composed of the concerned departments of the central and local governments should be set up to implement a permanent control over regional growth, while special committees could be set up to deal with the key issues in the construction of human settlements, such as the regional network of transportation, the preservation of water resources, the amelioration of regional environment, and the restructuring of regional economy.

1.4.2 Projects of Urban Planning and Design

• As case studies in the research of Sustainable Development of Human Settlements in the Northwest Area of Yunnan Province, several practical projects had been done at Zhongdian County, including the Master Plan of Zhongdian County, the Urban Design of the Town Center of Zhongdian, and the Preservation Plan of Jiantang Town in Zhongdian. The former was already approved by the provincial government and implemented at the end of 2000.

• Evaluation of the Master Plan of New Area of Suzhou and Detailed Plan for

Recent Actions, a project commissioned by the local government, which has been approved by the professional committee of experts.

1.4.3   Projects of Architectural Design

• Central Academy of Fine Arts: A project concerned the planning of the campus and the architectural design of 95,000 square meters. Named as one of the Ten Best Projects of Planning and Design of Beijing in 1996, this project was finished this autumn and has already been put into use.

• The Beijing Diaoyutai State Guesthouse site planning and design project was approved by the state government in 2000. Based on the project, a building number 19 architectural design scheme of 16,000 square meters has been completed.

• Institute of Confucius. Commissioned by the city government and Committee of Preservation of Cultural Relics of Qufu, this project deals with the conception of an architectural complex of 12,000 square meters. As one of the key projects in the Shandong Province, the first phase of construction was finished and the building was put into effect in 1999.

• Ecological Village in the city of Zhangjiagang. This is an international collaborative project with the Building and Social Housing Foundation of UK and the local government of Zhangjiagang. Two houses were constructed in 2000 and the environmental evaluation has been done this year.

• Beijing Housing 2000. This international collaborative project with our Korean colleagues is associated with the research of Spatial Development of the Region of Greater Beijing. Exemplary designs have been done in terms of housing rehabilitation and new housing prototypes and results were exhibited in Beijing in March 2001.

1.5   Conclusion

In 1993, based on the development situation, we felt couragous enough to set up the concept of Sciences of Human Settlements. By 2000, this concept became widely accepted in China.

Today, the great rural-urban development in China has seen unprecedented progress and its scale and amount rank first in the world. The achievements led us to think and research the Science of Human Settlements even self-conscious. We should keep the progress continuously and to guide the development on a proper route, and to search a new paradigm of tomorrow.

Urbanization, Sciences of Human Settlements, and the Practice of Urban Planning in China

Since the foundation of the People's Republic of China in 1949 and especially since the adoption of the policies of reform and opening up of the economy, China has obtained outstanding achievements in socio-economic development, as well as in urban and rural construction. Today, in terms of national economy, urban and rural construction accounts for about 7% of the annual GDP. Simultaneously, there has emerged a rather confusing phenomenon in China concerning urban and rural development. Although almost everyone has perceptual knowledge about building and a large amount of people are living in cities, only a few can provide clear definitions of architecture and city.

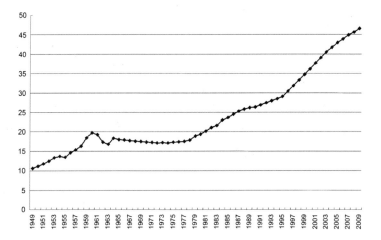

Fig. 2.1 Urbanization Process in China between 1949-2009

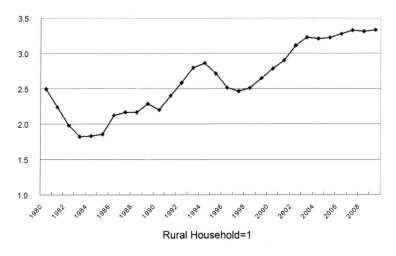

Rural Household=1

Fig. 2.2 China Urban-Rural Household Income Ration

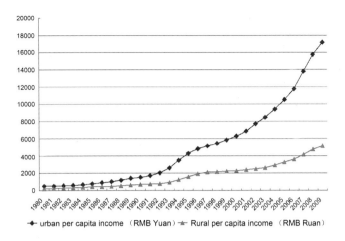

Fig. 2.3   China Urban-Rural Per Capita Income Between 1980-2009 (yuan RMB)

Today, under the circumstance of rapid urbanization, China faces different kinds of problems concerning urban and rural development, ranging from macroscopic problems, such as development strategies of a city, to microscopic problems such as implementation of building activities. Considering this fact, it is natural that there are arguments and criticisms from the public, to which the authorities concerned should pay due attention even though some of them might be partial or impertinent. However, for the administrative authorities, if the policies are made on the basis of unscientific concepts, the consequences might be catastrophic with irreversible results. This is why scientific urban policies are very important for the sound development of human settlements.

2.1   Urbanization: The Theme of the Age

In the new century, the pace of urbanization has progressed rapidly in China. An expert once predicted that the most influential events in the world at the beginning of the 21st Century would be the development of high-end technologies in the US and the urbanization of China. With regard to such a high speed of development, it is difficult to imagine what will take place in future in both the urban and rural areas of China. As uncountable new buildings and new facilities are constructed and many new cities and new city-regions emerge in China, it will be hard for us to make any comprehensive strategies for urban and rural development of China if we insist on the traditional concepts of architecture and city, i.e., to understand them only as isolated phenomenon instead of considering them as parts of urbanization.

In fact, there has already been a universal acknowledgement about urbanization in the international academic world. In the 1960s, the World Society for Ekistics (WSE) published a series of Delos Manifesto[1] based on extensive discussions, in which the issue of urbanization was addressed several times.

" *Urbanization is the result of development, and usually the burden of further development as well, but it should be also a measure to promote further development. Unfortunately, the promoting influence of urban growth on further development is not taken into consideration adequately.*" *(Delos One, 1963)*

" *By so far, people seldom, if not never, focus on the issue of urbanization, even that of housing. This situation which is equilibrating to the reality should be corrected and more efforts should be contributed to drafting policies of urbanization.*" *(Delos Two, 1964)*

At the same time, it proposed to establish the discipline of human settlements to deal with the problems of urbanization.

" *The forum restates the necessity to establish the discipline of human settlements which will target at showing the difficulties of human life under the new circumstances of changing and urbanization, solving the new problems of human settlements resulted from rapid changing by the way of integrating separate solutions into a comprehensive one.*" *(Delos Two, 1964)*

These theories are very enlightening for China. Actually, in the academic field of architecture and planning of the contemporary western countries, there are many insightful and foresighted scholars who have made their significant contributions to search for a sound road of development based on retrospections of the past, for example, from the perspectives of information technology, environment, ecology, and sustained development. After the reform and opening up in the 1980s, Chinese architects and planners tried their best to learn earnestly from their western counterparts

---

[1] Wu Liangyong. An Introduction to the Sciences of Human Settlements. China Architecture & Building Press. Beijing, October 2001. pp. 379-395.

and made outstanding contributions to the progress of urbanization in China.

Yet we must realize that under the condition of accelerating urbanization at such a high speed (with urbanization rate rising from 17.9% in 1978 to 41.8% by the end of 2004), China should not follow the western way in terms of urbanization strategies, especially that of the so-called American paradigm characterized by scattered cities, auto-mobilization, suburbanization, top-grade villas, skyscrapers, and so on. These phenomena should not be copied in China, not only because they would bring about consequential conflicts, but also because China cannot afford it. Today, China has to confront the shortage of resources, which are far from satisfactory for sustainable development. For example, when compared with the world average level, the water resource in China accounts for less than 25%, arable land for less than 40%, forest for 16.5%, petroleum for 8.3%, natural gas for 4.1% , and so on.

In addition, China has to deal with complicated social problems which emerge one after another during the procedure of development, for example, the problems of unemployment, housing, education, aging population, medical care, etc. There are also big concerns about the enlarging disparities in terms of wealth possession between different social estates, the considerable differences in terms of regional development between urban and rural areas, and the increasingly more interest conflicts resulting from the continuing polarization of social structure. All these problems are interconnected and unexpected, calling for serious considerations. Yet, when we try our best to search for possible solutions to deal with these problems, it is also urgent and essential for us to explore the theories of architecture and city, which will serve as guidelines to the future development of architecture and city. We should recognize that the western experiences of urbanization do not present us with ready answers and we have to therefore seek a unique road of urbanization for China with close accordance to the specific conditions in the country.

2.2 Development of Sciences of Human Settlements

As serious scholars with a scientific attitude, we pressingly recognize that our academic researches on urban and rural development are still deficient and the existing disciplines of architecture and urban planning are incapable of providing comprehensive and efficient solutions to practical issues. At present, though many disciplines are involved in large-scale constructions taking place in both urban and rural areas, they are not based on universally acknowledged professional guidance and they do not coordinate with one another to achieve common goals. Therefore, when confronted with the demands of development of the new era, it is urgent for Chinese scholars to develop new academic concepts, dealing with the issues of human settlements, society, and environment in a comprehensive and holistic way.

Enlightened by the concept of "human settlements" and "habitat", I put forward in 1989 the "General Theory of Architecture" in my manuscript with the same title, marking the start of my research on the sciences of human settlements. In August 1993, together with my copartners, I proposed to establish the "Sciences of Human Settlements" [1] during a seminar organized by the Department of Science of Technology, Chinese Academy of Sciences. In 2001, I published another manuscript entitled "Introduction to the Sciences of Human Settlements" and gave a lecture at the annual meeting of WSE held in Berlin in October of the same year with the title "Theoretical & Practical Explorations for Sciences of Human Settlements". [2]

Along with the general trends of urban and rural development in China in the recent years, I tried to enrich my academic theories in the following aspects.

2.2.1　Urbanization vs. "Five Balanced Aspects"

Recently, "promoting the process of urbanization" has become an important issue in China and it is the first time in the history of China that such great attention is being paid to research on urbanization. This is a good trend. As stated in the Istanbul Charter of the Habitat Ⅱ of UN in 1996, "urban and rural developments

---

[1] Wu Liangyong, Zhou Ganzhi, Lin Zhiqun. Today and Tomorrow of Building Industry of China. Beijing: City Press, 1994.

[2] Wu Liangyong. Sciences of Human Settlements: Searching for the Theory and Practice. Ekistics. 415, 416, 417, July/August, September/October, November/December, 2002.

are correlated. In addition to improving the living environments in urban areas, we should make great efforts to increase appropriate infrastructures, public service establishments, and employment opportunities in rural areas so as to enhance the attraction of countryside. We should develop unified residential networks to reduce the rural-to-urban migrations."

In 2003, the Chinese Government brought forward the new concept of "Five Balanced Aspects", namely, "balancing urban and rural development, balancing regional development, balancing social and economic development, balancing human and natural development, and balancing domestic development and opening to the outside world". These five aspects can be regarded as an intensive summarization of the achievements and the problems as well of construction in China in the past half-century. They can serve as general guidelines for the socio-economic development of China, as well as the top principles for the development of human settlements in China. Thus, great attention should be paid to this new concept. On the one hand, we should seriously retrospect on the work we have done with accordance to these guidelines; while on the other hand, we should consciously implement these political creeds in our technical practice.

Thus, I further developed my theories of Sciences of Human Settlements and revised the basic research grid of Sciences of Human Settlements, which is composed of "Five Principles" (i.e., principles of ecology, economy, technology, society, and culture and art), "Five Elements" (i.e., nature, human beings, society, settlements, and supporting network), and "Five Levels" (i.e., world, region, city, community, and building). "Five Balanced Aspects" (i.e., balancing urban and rural development, balancing regional development, balancing social and economic development, balancing human and natural development, and balancing domestic development and opening to the outside world) is set on the dominant level of the grid, serving as the top principles of the Sciences of Human Settlements.

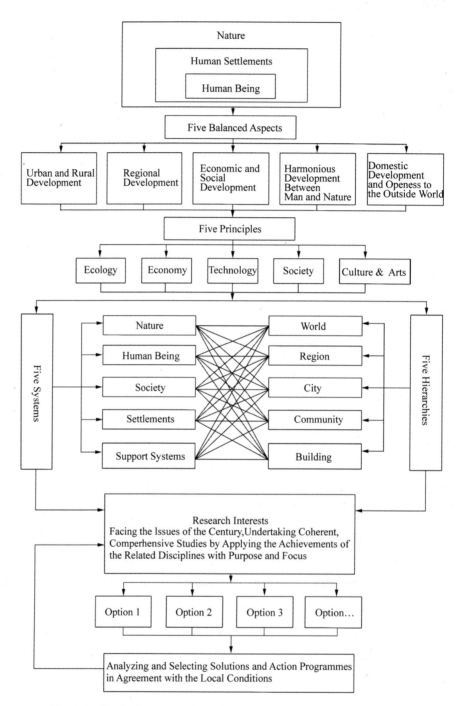

Fig. 2.4 Basic Research Grid of Sciences of Human Settlements

2.2.2 Urban and Rural Development vs. Construction of New Countryside

In his dedication for the World Habitat Day in 2004, Kofi Annan, Secretary-General of the United Nations stated that,"The theme of World Habitat Day this year, Cities – engines of rural development, was chosen to remind development policy makers at every level not to think of 'urban'and 'rural'as separate entities, but rather as parts of an economic and social whole. Cities interact with rural areas in many ways."

It is enlightened in the report of "Suggestions on drafting the 11th Five-Year-Plan for National Economic and Social Development" delivered by the Central Committee of the Communist Party of China that, "positive efforts should be made to promote the balanced development of urban and rural areas. Building new socialist countryside is an important historical task during the modernization of China. The building of new country should be carried out firmly and steadily following the requirements of growing production, prosperous life, civilized atmosphere, clean appearance, and democratic management, and with accordance to specific local conditions and farmers' real wills." "A long-term effective mechanism should be established to encourage the reversed feeding of industry to agriculture and city to countryside. Due attention should be paid to construction planning of countryside."

Although city and rural area are inevitably different from each other and different methods and policies should be adapted to deal with problems of urban and rural development respectively, neither of them could be emphasized nor ignored partially for achieving the final goal of sustainable development. We should realize that the prosperity of rural area is an important base for sound urbanization and urbanization should never be at the cost of the decline of agriculture and the lagging modernization of countryside. It is possible as well as necessary that urban development makes its significant contribution to the prosperity of rural development.

Currently, we are trying our best to explore the building of a new socialist countryside. Based on the experiences and lessons learnt from historic practices (for example, those carried out by the students and staffs of Tsinghua University in 1959 [1]),

---

[1] In 1959, the staffs and students of Department of Architecture, Tsinghua University were involved in the design and construction of the residential community at Shangzhuang People' s Commune, Xushui County, Hebei Province. Since the ordinary building materials were not affordable there at that time, all the two- or three-storied building were constructed in reed which had to be demolished late on.

we believe that the prosperity of countryside relies on the comprehensive development of agriculture, processing industry of agricultural products, education, medical care, housing, socialized services, as well as construction of towns and villages.

2.2.3 Integration and Exploitation of Architecture, Urban Planning, and Landscape Architecture from Regional Perspective

According to my theories of Sciences of Human Settlements, the integrity of architecture, urban planning, and landscape architecture (or the so-called "triplicity") is the core of the Sciences of Human Settlements. Today, with regard to the construction practice in the developed coastal areas of China, it is not enough to keep our minds only on cities. Instead, more attention should be paid to dealing with the interrelationship among urban, suburban, and rural areas in terms of transportation and spatial development, the protection of ecologic environment and landscape resources, the opening up of recreational areas, and so on. Thus, it is necessary to further promote the integration and exploitation of architecture, urban planning, and landscape architecture (please refer to the following two diagrams).

2.2.4 Research on and Application of Methodologies

From the perspective of methodology, the object with which the above academic framework deals is "an open and complicated mega-system". To some extent, we are engaging in creative research with holistic thinking and concepts of science of complexity.

Generally speaking, the development of Sciences of Human Settlements in China is still in its initial state and we are still working hard to search for the unique way of China with accordance to the realities of China, getting ideas from relevant disciplines, taking lessons and drawing experiences from domestic and overseas advanced practices.

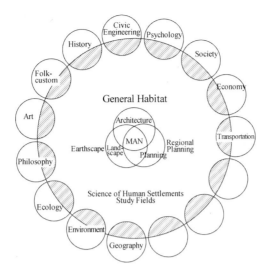

Fig. 2.5   Sciences of Human Settlements: Creating an Open System (1996)

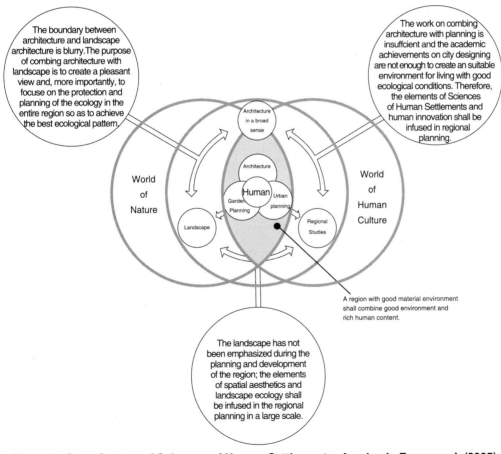

Fig. 2.6   Open System of Sciences of Human Settlements: Academic Framework (2005)

2.3 Theoretical Application of Sciences of Human Settlements in the Practice of Urban and Rural Planning in China

Personally, I have tried to apply the theories of Sciences of Human Settlements in my systematic practice of urban and rural planning in China and have developed them continuously through the practice. With the "problem-oriented" methodology, I enlarged my practical scope progressively from architecture to urban studies and further to regional and cultural studies, which could be classified into the following three platforms.

2.3.1 Platform One: Exploration for New Paradigms of Urban Development Based on the Concept of "Regional Block"

(1) Theory of "City-Region": To research for spatial development strategies of city-regions from regional perspective to achieve coordinated regional development

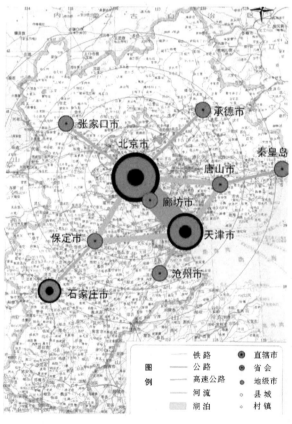

Fig. 2.7 Greater Beijing Region (Beijing-Tianjin-Tangshan-Baoding and Surrounding)

and co-prosperity of big, medium-sized, and small cities, as well as towns and villages. Our research work on the Yangtze River Delta Region, the Pearl River Delta Region, the Northwestern Yunnan and Greater Beijing Region are pioneering works of architects on spatial development strategies and urban system of city-regions.

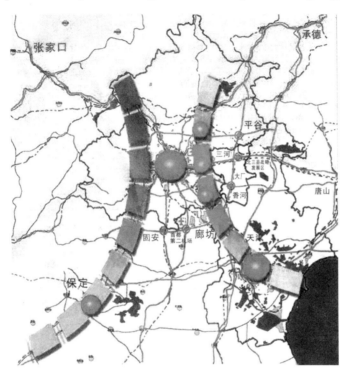

Fig. 2.8 Beijing Two-Belt Strategy Spatial

Fig. 2.9 Beijing Urban Proper Planning Pattern

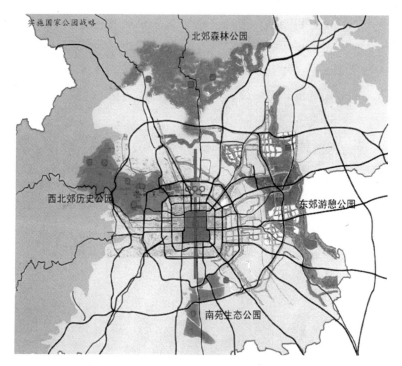

Fig. 2.10　Beijing National Park Strategy

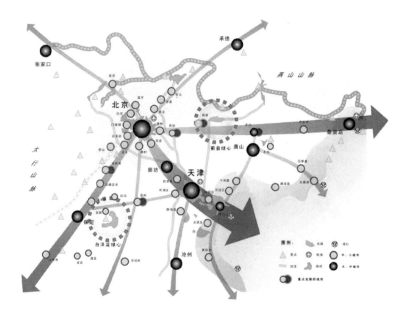

Fig. 2.11　Greater Beijing Spatial Development Strategic Plan

(2) Theory of "Regional Architecture". At the beginning of the 1980s, I put forward the theory of regional architecture and advocated in 1988 the modernization of regional architecture and regionalization of modern architecture. My designs for Confucius Institute in Qufu and Museum of Mount Tai in Tai'an, Shandong Province can be regarded as practical implementation of regional architecture.

Fig. 2.12　Master Plan of Tai'an City

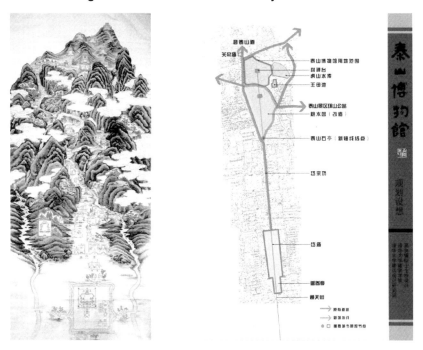

Fig. 2.13　Taishan Museum Design – 1　Fig. 2.14　Taishan Museum Design – 2

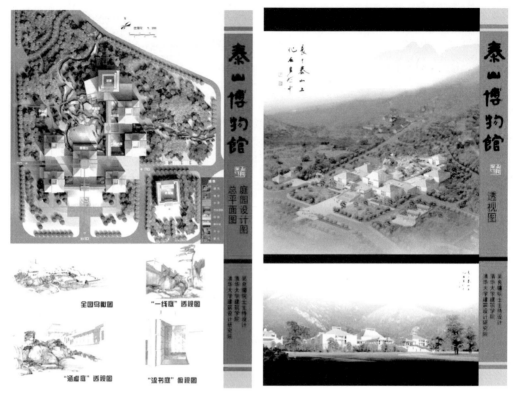

Fig. 2.15　Taishan Museum Design – 3　　**Fig. 2.16　Taishan Museum Design – 4**

(3) Theory of "Regional-Scape or/and Earth-Scape". This refers to enlarging the scope of landscape from gardens of micro-level to regions and even the earth of macro-level. My proposals of "four national park strategy" for Beijing and "Quehua National Park" for Jinan are guided by the theory of regional-scape.

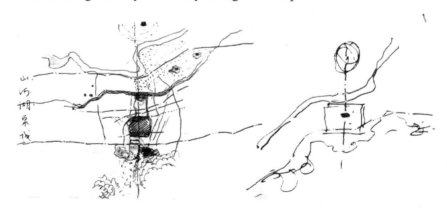

Fig. 2.17　Jinan City Scape and Landscape, Sketch by Wu Liangyong

Fig. 2.18   The picture of Que and Hua mountain in autumn (Zhao Mengfu , Yuan Dynasty)

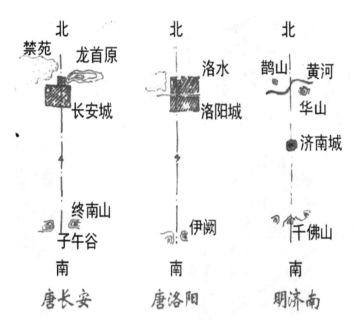

Fig. 2.19   Jinan City Axis to Compare with Changan and Luoyang, Sketch by Wu Liangyong

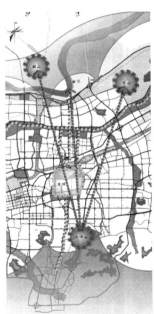

Fig. 2.20   Jinan City's Viewpoint from the Qianfo Mount

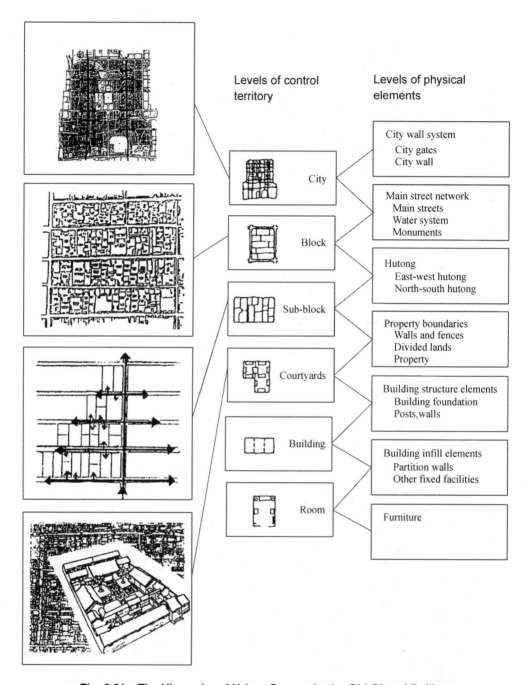

Fig. 2.21   The Hierarchy of Urban Spaces in the Old City of Beijing

Fig. 2.22   Beijing Ju'er Hutong before Renovation

Fig. 2.23   Beijing Ju'er Hutong New Courtyard Housing Project – 1

Fig. 2.24   Beijing Ju'er Hutong New Courtyard Housing Project – 2

2.3.2   Platform Two: Concepts of "Urban Unit" and "Design Module" to Create Relative Integrity during the Process of Development

I insist that architectural design should be done with holistic thinking of urban design, focusing not only on restructuring urban fabric or urban order, but also thinking about improving the system of civil infrastructure. When designing, each site of a city should be regarded as an "urban unit" and be treated as a "design module" so as to achieve integral harmony out of chaos.

(1) A city could be divided into many urban units of design with accordance to not only functional differentiation, but also natural situations or built-up elements.

(2) The planning and design of an urban unit should firstly "connect the preceding and the following", which means to conform to the requirements of the higher-level planning while providing guidelines for the lower-level planning; secondly "glance right and left", which means to consider the relationships with its neighbors; and thirdly "conceive future", which means to forecast as much as possible

the changes of life in the future and to explore as much as possible spaces to hold the potential growth.

(3) The objective in terms of physical environment is to achieve the beauty of integral coordination, which means to create order within chaos and harmony of difference.

2.3.3   Platform Three: Comprehensive Innovation with Cultural Connotations

This refers to the development of new paradigms on the basis of summarizing historic experiences, grasping fundamental laws, and meditating on original prototypes.

(1) We should learn from the successful experiences in human history all over the world and create a regional architecture full of local characters all over China.

(2) Under the circumstances of economic globalization and cultural diversification, due attention should be paid coequally to global culture and local culture. In terms of either global perspective or local action, none of them should be partially ignored or discarded.

(3) Concerning the development of architecture, science and culture should be highlighted coequally. On the one hand, we should establish the concept of "great science" to learn and apply sciences in architecture; while on the other hand, we should have the concept of "great art" to integrate architecture with painting, sculpture, and fine arts to enhance the artful expression of architecture, to create the soul of architecture of the era and to intensify the cultural connotations of the built environment.

2.4   Conclusion

All my theoretical and practical works, including manuscripts, dissertations, as well as planning and design works are elements of my designing knowledge system, which aims at integrating science with humanism. One thing needs to be clarified here that, although till now my theoretical and practical works are confirmed by some colleagues, both domestically and overseas, I still think that they represent only one school of thought. In China, we have an ancient philosophical saying, "There might be one hundred different ideas for one object, and there might be one hundred different ways for one destination". In other words, a common road as well as a common destination could be found even when confronted with numerous problems. This is what I refer to as problem-oriented. As Chinese architects, we should try our best to explore different ways and put forward different ideas to find out a common direction leading to the common goal, that is, to develop the school of Chinese architecture.

Transformation of Development Mode and Exploration on Sciences of Human Settlements

Advanced sciences and technologies created industrial civilization, unprecedentedly bringing about tremendous productivity and greatly promoting urban and rural development, as well as leading to unparalleled crises in human settlements. Learning from development experiences in the past, today, human society has realized that the development mode must be changed to fit new situations. This is applicable for the Sciences of Human Settlements, which should also be further developed to meet the requirements of new situations.

3.1 Development Mode in the 19th and 20th Centuries and Three Main Themes of Exploration on Human Settlements

3.1.1 Awareness of Environmental Issues and Perception of Development Mode in the West

In the west, advanced sciences and technologies created splendid industrial civilization, and the changes of production relations released unprecedentedly the enormous productivity. The industrialization in the 19th and 20th centuries facilitated the process of urbanization and the rise of large cities; while the damages that the "Paleo-technique Era" have done to the environment have also accelerated today's environmental crises.

3.1.1.1 Damages of "Paleo-technique Era" to Environment and Environmental Crises

The influences of industrialization and urbanization on environment began gradually aggravating, with serious public hazards occurring again and again. Only when environmental deterioration began to threaten man's health, did human society commonly acknowledge the existence of environmental issues.

After the 1950s, several environmental disasters occurred across the world, and the oil crisis of 1973 also provided human society with a series of warnings. In 1972, the "Declaration on Human Environment" was adopted at the Stockholm Conference, putting forward the warning of "only one earth". Since then, worldwide attention to environment has led to the rise of "Environment Science". Twenty years later, the world summit meeting – Rio Conference on Environment and Development – was held in 1992, approving the "Agenda 21"despite different opinions.

3.1.1.2 Awakening the Awareness of Human Settlements

Along with the rapid process of urbanization, the proportion of urban population in the world population has been constantly increasing, being 3% in 1800, 13% in 1900, and soaring to 47% in 2000. Currently, about half of the world population is living in cities and towns, and the rate is estimated to reach about two-thirds in the next 30 years. Under such a circumstance, how can we realize environment-friendly and sustainable growth and the development of cities? Some insightful thinkers, politicians, scholars, as well as architects and planners started to actively explore the way for future development. The awareness of human settlements has thus been awakened in the whole world.

In 1933, the International Congress of Modern Architecture was held in Athens, approving the meaningful document of the Athens Charter. In the following 10 years, J. Sert tried his best to work on the materials that he presented during the congress and published them in the book titled "Can Our Cities Survive"?, warning the world about the dangers that human society faced.

After I read this book in 1947, it became the slender sunlight in the morning that oriented my academic work. Later on, represented by the Greek scholar C. Doxiadis and in line with the principles of Athens Charter, a series of meetings were held on the Delos Island in the Aegean Sea, during which the concept of Ekistics was formed. Owing to the efforts of Doxiadis and others, the United Nations Conference on Human Settlements was held in Vancouver in 1976.

Twenty years later, the importance of human settlements was further recognized in the world. In 1996, the United Nations Conference on Human Settlements (Habitat II) was held in Istanbul, adopting the Istanbul Declaration on Human Settlements and the Habitat Agenda. In 2001, the conference of "Istanbul+5" was held in New York, approving the Declaration on Cities and Other Human Settlements in the New Millennium. In the same year, according to the decision of the United Nations General Assembly, the United Nations Commission on Human Settlements (Habitat) was transformed into the United Nations Human Settlements Programme (UN-HABITAT) that was endowed with stronger competence of fund-raising and coordination.

Since then, the UN-HABITAT has collaborated with the United Nations Environment Programme (UNEP) that was founded in 1973, playing a more and more important role in promoting the development of human settlements. The work of "environment" and "human settlements" has been gradually carried out, focusing particularly on the issues of environment and human settlements of the grass-roots in developing countries.

3.1.1.3　Hard-Won Concept of Sustainable Development

In the first half of the 20th Century, influenced by the academic works of Lewis Patrick Geddes published in 1915, the insightful American scholar Lewis Mumford advocated that, by breaking away from the isolated academic routes of specialists, the issue of "human environment" should be studied through a comprehensive observation of various phenomena. He criticized the development mode after the industrial revolution, which he named as "Paleo-technique Era"[1], and expected the arrival of the era of "biotechnology order".

After the preparation of about 50 years, the tiny streams of thoughts finally converged into a mighty torrent. In 1987, the World Commission on Environment and Development (WCED) put forward the concept of "sustainable development"[2] in the report of Our Common Future, forming the common understanding of the whole mankind and the common outline that must be observed by the whole world. In recent years, there have emerged constantly new achievements of researches on sustainable development in the world. For instance, Canadian scholars proposed the concept of

---

[1] The two books of Technics and Civilization (1934) and Culture of Cities (1938) by Lewis Mumford involve the discussions on the mode of technological development.

[2] On Apr. 27, 1987, the World Commission on Environment and Development (WCED) published the report of "Our Common Future", putting forward the strategic thought of "sustainable development" and its definition. The so-called "sustainable development" is the development that can not only meet people's needs of the contemporary era, but will also not impair the competences of future generations to satisfy their needs.

"Ecological Footprint" **❶** in 1996, appealing to mankind to relieve the heavy burden on the earth.

In 2001, Klaus Toepfer, the Executive Director of UNEP, pointed out in his statement the 10 environmental hazards that human beings are facing, i.e., soil destruction, climate change and energy waste, loss of biological diversity, reduction of forest, threatened fresh water resources, industrial pollution, chaotic urbanization, over-exploitation of ocean and pollution of coast, and air pollution and depletion of the stratospheric ozone layer.

In May 2005, the United Nations published the Appraisal Report on Biological Environment in the Millennium, which was jointly completed by 1,300 scholars and experts from 95 countries. The report states that, for half a century, human activities have caused great harm to the biological environment of the earth, which will threaten the long-term development of mankind. At present, 10% ~ 30% of the rare wild animals are near extinction, and 15 of the 24 biological systems are worsening continuously. According to the report, if the current situation of deterioration continues, the biological environment may see a sudden revolution, resulting in the change of quality of water resources, the spread of new diseases, the death of marine organisms along the coasts, and the abnormal change of climate.

In October 2006, a 700-page report of the British Government compiled by Nicholas Stern, the former Executive Economist of World Bank, stated that if the government of each country does not take measures to control the greenhouse effect in the next 10 years, an economic cost as high as USD 6.98 trillion will be incurred worldwide, which surpasses the total cost of the two World Wars and the Depression of the US in the 1930s. Then, most of the earth will become unlivable for mankind, and about 200 million people will become "environmental refugees" because of drought or food shortage.

In summary, from discovering the environmental issues and acknowledging the importance of human environment, to awakening the awareness of human settlements, and then to achieving the common understanding of sustainable development, the three

---

❶ M. Wachernagel and W. Rees. Our Ecological Footprint – Reducing Human Impact on the Earth, 1996.

events can be regarded as the three major themes in the field of physical environment construction since the 19th Century. It deserves particular attention that the concept of sustainable development brings the prospect of a new development mode in the 21st Century.

3.1.2 China's Reconsideration on Development Mode

Since the 1950s, while it continues to learn from the former Soviet Union and the west, China has gradually realized that it should explore its own way of development based on its specific situations. The exploration process is inevitably tough for various reasons, and the development path of promoting diversified technologies for rapid socio-economic development was not found until China's reform and opening-up to the outside world in the 1980s. Summing up the development progress of China in the last 30 years, it can still be concluded into the three main themes of environmental issues, human settlements, and development mode.

3.1.2.1 Environmental Crises

With a large population, China has a long history of territorial development, leaving a relatively small room for future development. For instance, the area from Boston to New York and Washington, which was classified as megalopolis by Jean Gottmann, is just a series of cities isolated in an open field; while in southern Jiangsu Province of China, cities and towns are connected with one another, forming an urban agglomeration where the respective boundary is hard to be identified. As the town density in southern Jiangsu is incomparable with that of the megalopolises in the US, environmental issues are more urgent here and the contradiction between population, resources, and environment is more severe.

Land Resources: In China, the arable land is only 13% of the whole territory in terms of area, and the arable land per capita is merely 1.43 mu ❶, less than 40% of

---

❶ Editor's note: "Mu" is a Chinese unit of area. One mu is equal to 1/15 hectare.

the world average. [1] "In the Yangtze Valley, the arable land per capita is only 0.84 mu, which is close to the warning line of 0.8 mu set by the UN Food and Agriculture Organization (FAO). The soil erosion intensifies further the already fierce conflicts between man and land. The loss of arable land even threatens our survival, because it destroys the foundation of sustainable development of agriculture and then menaces the grain safety of the country."

Water Resources: In China, the water resource per capita is 2,200 m^3, which is only a quarter of the world average [2]. About one-sixth of Chinese cities suffer from serious water shortage, and five major city clusters are in overuse of water resources. Water resources are badly destroyed due to improper sewage disposal, with only 41% of the seven major water systems being of the water quality of I to III categories, and 32% of IV to V categories, 37% of worse than the V category, all of which lead to shortage of drinking water for human life.

Energy Resources: Regarding the energy consumption of buildings in China, 95% of the existing floor area of 40 billion square meters is of high-energy-consumption buildings. Among the annual increase of floor area of 2 billion square meters, 80% are of the high-energy-consumption category. For making the solid bricks used for construction, about 120,000 mu farmland is destroyed every year, and the water consumption of sanitaryware is more than 30% higher than that in the developed countries [3].

Environment: In China, air pollution has spread from cities to the countryside, with the concentration of fine particles and that of ozone being increased, which results in widespread haze. The long-standing environmental pollution in cities still continues, leading to the frequently happening crises such as the pollution of Tuojiang River in 2003, that of Huaihe River in 2004, that of Songhuajiang River in 2005 caused by the pollutant emission from the Jilin Chemical Plant, the blue-green algae event of Taihu

---

[1] "The arable land is only 13% of the whole territory in terms of area. It was 1.95 billion mu in 1996, and 1.85 billion at the end of 2006, being reduced by 0.1 billion in seven years. Currently, the arable land per capita of China is merely 1.43 mu, less than 40% of the world average." Speech of WANG Guangtao on the national conference on village and town construction on Jul. 8, 2004.

[2] Speech of LIAO Chunyan on the Annual Conference of China Association For Science and Technology 2007 held in Wuhan on Sept. 13, 2007.

[3] Quoted from QIU Baoxing, Deputy Minister of Construction.

Lake in 2007, as well as that of Dianchi Lake and Chaohu Lake. Moreover, there also exist the pollutions of sludge and fertilizer, which have not been fully noticed.

The conflicts between population, resources, and environment aggravate the complication of the issues of urban and rural human settlements in China. Based on the current development mode, how much carrying capacity do Chinese cities and regions still have? What should be the development path in future? In view of issues such as concentrated population, congested traffic, deteriorated environment, and endangered ecological safety caused by the rapid socio-economic development and urbanization, the rational carrying capacity of human settlements has attracted more and more attention [1]. Recently, WU Jinglian pointed out in a paper that, from the perspective of socio-economic life, there are two most urgent problems: one is the aggravation of resource shortage and environmental pollution, and the other is the deterioration of social environment [2].

Reviewing the development in the past and analyzing the situation at present, it can be seen that once a wrong decision concerning man's living environment is taken, it will lead to serious mistakes that are hard to reverse. For example, in Kunming, the farmland reclamation around the Dianchi Lake during the Culture Revolution and the waterfront development later on have resulted in a series of problems, which should be remembered forever.

3.1.2.2 Human Settlements

Up to now, environmental crises have been commonly acknowledged by the academic field, the whole society, as well as the decision-makers, who have made great efforts to ameliorate the situation. The problems of human settlements still exist widely, such as the issues of housing, ecology, and transport, which call for the exploration and the new expression of academic concepts. In China, the densely urbanized areas such as the Yangtze River Delta and the Pearl River Delta are usually the places where high-

---

[1] For example, the worldwide common understanding of sustainable development and the concept of ecological carrying capacity like Rees' theory of "Ecological Footprint", which are put forward to deal with the problems caused by the traditional development mode of the west. China Association For Science and Technology. Report on Carrying Capacity of Chinese Cities and Crisis Management, 2007.

[2] WU Jinglian. Difficulties of China's Economic Transformation and Their Solutions. Feb. 4, 2008. <http://www.enorth.com.cn>.

quality farmlands are concentrated. Thus, the damage of any kind of construction to the natural environment will bring about more severe problems in greater cost. However, in reality, the natural laws are usually violated for achieving faster development. For instance, as large-scale constructions call for a large amount of funds, the overseas investments are often introduced; meanwhile, a large sum of land is inevitably used in hope of the remarkable GDP growth and the "outstanding" and distinctive projects of "political credits". Nevertheless, the time when these projects are completed, is also the time when the original city features disappear.

The 17th National Congress of the Communist Party of China (CPC) pointed out that in China, "The economic growth is realized at an excessively high cost of resources and environment. There remains an imbalance of development between city and county, among different regions, and between economy and society. It becomes more difficult to assure a steady growth of agriculture and a continued increase of farmers' income. There exist still many problems affecting people's immediate interests in the areas such as employment, social guarantee, income distribution, education, health care, housing, work safety, justice and public security and so on. Some low-income residents are still in a rather difficult life.

In fact, the factors influencing the important policies of China are all related to the issue of human settlements. The constructions of economy, polity, culture, and society of both the country and the locality need to be carried out in a coordinated fashion in space, forming the "spatial development strategies" and thus facilitating the healthy development of human settlements. The sound development of the academic theories of human settlements is beneficial to the establishment of the strategies of spatial development and the policies of human settlements as well. In terms of planning, the concept of human settlements should be taken as a necessary content in the territorial, regional, and urban planning.

3.1.2.3 Scientific View of Development – The Development Path Based on China's Reality

Compared with the west, China's socio-economic development and urbanization are larger in scale and faster, but it falls behind in terms of awareness of the problems concerned and the studies on technologies. Yet, the development mode of the west, including those which have already been proven to be improper for China, is being used in China.

Therefore, apart from drawing lessons from the experience of the west, it is necessary for us to seek a path different from that of the west, i.e., a development path specific to China. The Scientific View of Development is proposed in view of China's fundamental realities in the primary stage of socialism, the summarization of China's development practice, the development experience of foreign countries, and the new development requirements of the time.

The Scientific View of Development is elaborated on the 17th National Congress of CPC as follows: "The Scientific View of Development takes development as its essence, humanism as its core, comprehensive, balanced, and sustainable development as its basic requirements, and overall consideration as its fundamental approach."

The Scientific View of Development, as the hard-won strategic guideline and the basic direction for China's development path, should be carried out in the Sciences of Human Settlements.

3.1.3   Development of Sciences of Human Settlements

3.1.3.1   Exploration on Sciences of Human Settlements

Human settlement, as the name implies, is the place that humans inhabit and the territory where human activities take place. These settlements are the bases on which mankind rely for existence, as well as the sites where mankind utilize and renovate nature.

As mentioned before, it took mankind quite a long time to become aware of the issue of human settlements, for example, Lewis Mumford put forward the concept of "human environment" in the 1930s, C. Doxiadis proposed the concept of Ekistics in the 1950s, and the concept of "Human Habitat" emerged much later. In China, the knowledge of human settlements comes from not only overseas theories, but also its own creation. From 1985 to 2001, WU Liangyong established gradually his thoughts on the Sciences of Human Settlements.

In August 1993, in their speech on the academia seminar organized by the Science and Technology Department of Chinese Academy of Sciences, WU Liangyong, ZHOU Ganzhi, and LIN Zhiqun discussed the relationship between construction and socio-economic development, and put forward the new academic concept and system of "Sciences of Human Settlements" in view of the unprecedented conflicts and problems caused by China's socio-economic development of unprecedented scale and speed in the 1980s, i.e., to establish and develop a group of disciplines that is based on the environment and the living and working activities of mankind and focusing on the "protection and development" of the man-made and natural environment ranging from buildings to cities and towns. Instead of being limited to a single discipline, it is a new generalized and comprehensive disciplinary system that integrates all the sciences, including natural science, technology science, and humanity, which are concerned with the formation and development of human settlements. This was the first time that the concept was officially put forward to the public [1]. In 2001, WU Liangyong published the monograph of "Introduction to Sciences of Human Settlements", which discusses the possible development goals of human settlements, analyzes the different solutions and guidelines that are suitable to the conditions of different regions, and proposes many research frameworks, thus laying down the academic basis for the further development of Sciences of Human Settlements in China [2].

Today along with the globalization of society and economy, China's knowledge of human settlements has gradually developed from focusing on the concept of "environment" in the early stage to the "spatial" connotations of economy, society, biology, etc., as well as to the more profound contents such as regional cultures.

3.1.3.2 Human Settlements Already Becoming One of the Main Contents of China's Construction

Owing to the arduous exploration of the academic fields of both China and abroad

---

[1] WU Liangyong, ZHOU Ganzhi, and LIN Zhiqun. Present and Future of China's Construction Cause. Beijing: China City Press, 1994. Science and Technology Department of the Chinese Academy of Sciences. Present and Future of China's Construction Cause (Abstract). Bulletin of Chinese Academy of Sciences, 1994, 2.

[2] WU Liangyong. Introduction to Sciences of Human Settlements. Beijing: China Architecture & Building Press, 2001.

for many years, the development of human settlements has become an important part of the country's construction.

In March 2001, the Outline of the 10th Five-Year Plan pointed out in the part titled "Establishing Rationally Urban System" that, "Focusing on creating better human settlements, efforts should be made to enhance the ecological construction and the comprehensive treatment of pollutions in cities and towns so as to improve the environment. Planning, design, construction, and overall administration of cities and towns should be promoted so as to form the distinctive urban identities and to improve the urban administration level in an all-around way."This was the first time that the concept of "human settlements" was stated in the official document of the country.

In July 2003, China's Guidelines of Sustainable Development in Early 21st Century drafted by the National Development and Reform Commission pointed out in the chapter of "Urbanization and Construction of Small Cities" that, "Due efforts should be made to enhance the construction of urban infrastructures, to promote the employment in cities and towns, and to complete the functions of cities and towns including housing, public service, social service, and so on. Meanwhile, it should highlight the community administration in cities so as to build the new orderly, civilized, and harmonious urban communities and create better human settlements, and strengthen the comprehensive administration of cities and towns so as to form the distinctive urban identity and to improve the administration level of cities and towns in an all-around way."

On October 11, 2005, the Proposal of CPC Central Committee for Formulating the 11th Five-Year Plan of National Socio-Economic Development pointed out in the part entitled "Promoting Healthy Development of Urbanization" that, "Efforts should be made to carry out regional planning, urban planning, and land-use planning in a coordinated way, so as to improve the human settlements, maintain the local features, and promote the urban administration level."

On December 31, 2005, the Opinions of CPC Central Committee and State Council on Promoting New Socialist Countryside Construction (Central Committee Document No. 1 of 2006) required to "enhance village planning and renovate human settlements".

On January 29, 2007, the Opinions of CPC Central Committee and State Council on Actively Developing Modern Agriculture and Substantially Promoting New Socialist Countryside Construction (Central Committee Document No. 1 of 2007) required to "renovate the human settlements in the countryside, promote the planning and the experiment of village renovation, and save the rural construction land."

On October 15, 2007, President HU Jintao stated in his speech during the 17th National Congress of CPC entitled "Holding High Great Banner of Socialism with Chinese Characteristics and Striving for New Victories in Building a Moderately Prosperous Society in all Respects" that, "Due efforts should be made to increase the investment in energy-saving and environmental protection, with focus on intensifying the prevention and control of water, air, and soil pollutions, so as to improve the human settlements in both cities and counties."

On December 31, 2007, the Opinions of CPC Central Committee and State Council on Enhancing Agricultural Construction and Further Promoting Agricultural Development and Increase of Farmers' Income (Central Committee Document No. 1 of 2008) required that "it should continue to improve the human settlements in the countryside".

In view of the frequent occurrence of the phrase "human settlements" in many documents of the Chinese Central Government, it can be seen that the development of human settlements has already become an important part of China's construction, which has profound influences on the socio-economic development of the country.

3.2　New Opportunities and Challenges

3.2.1　Accelerated Scientific and Technological Revolution and Economic Globalization

Nowadays, the world is in the process of large-scale transformation and restructuring. Peace and development are still the themes of this era, and the pursuit of peace, the striving for development, and the promotion of cooperation have become irresistible tendencies. The further development of economic globalization and the acceleration of scientific and technological revolution will both have significant influences on the development of mankind and the construction of human settlements.

The above-mentioned influences are always two-faced. Taking culture as an example, on the one hand, they can help to have the perspective of cultural development in the world, to raise the levels of productivity and culture of the region, to improve the competitiveness of the city, and to promote the rank of the city in the national and global urban systems. On the other hand, regarding the substantial and insubstantial heritages of the locality, including local customs and features, they might be finally damaged if they cannot be well preserved and developed. The modern aesthetic fashion featured by the so-called global modernity and dominated by technicism tends to eliminate the regional features of architectural culture and folk culture, which has already affected local cultures to a different extent.

With the gradual development of economic globalization, few cities or regions can be free from the direct or indirect influences of globalization. Some western scholars hold the view that at present, the role of local governments is changing from the highest governor to enterprise [1]. Although this statement is not absolutely correct, it at least reveals the impacts of economic globalization on localities. We should notice the opportunities brought by the global capital entering the market, which, if well used, could play an active part in the local development. Meanwhile, we should pay due attention to the scramble of land as a kind of "spatial capital" for development, which, as some intelligent scholars have pointed out, might cause disasters if not handled properly.

Currently, the relationship between China and the world is changing dramatically, with China's future and destiny being more closely related to that of the world. Yet, one of the influences brought about by economic globalization is the impact on local cultures, which leads to the loss of the spirit of local and national cultures. For instance, in Beijing, although the protection of courtyard houses has already been regulated for many years, the destructions continue without end. Together with the appearance of the abnormal buildings everywhere, they result in the fading away of the charm of the ancient cultural city, which deserves our deep contemplation.

---

[1] A. Orum and CHEN Xiangming. The World of Cities – Places in Comparative and Historical Perspective, 2003.

3.2.2 Accelerated Urbanization in the World

At present, the world is undergoing the fastest population migration and urbanization in human history. How to minimize the aggravating poverty in cities? How to improve the urban poor's access to basic facilities such as shelter, clean water and sanitation, so as to achieve environment-friendly and sustainable urban growth and development? Along with demographic growth and population migration, can all the people obtain services like job, housing, water, electricity, and medicare? Can we satisfy their basic requirements even if we cannot meet all the needs of all the people?

Established by the UN, the World Urban Forum is dedicated to examining one of the most pressing issues facing the world today, i.e., the rapid urbanization and its impacts on communities, cities, economies, and policies. The Forum is held once every two years in different cities with different themes, for example the Nairobi Forum in 2002 with the theme of "Sustainable Urbanization"; the Barcelona Forum in 2004 with the theme of "Cities: Crossroad of culture, Inclusiveness, and Integration?"; and the Vancouver Forum in 2006 with the theme "Sustainable Cities: Turning Ideas into Action". In October 2008, the forum was held in Nanjing with the theme of "Harmonious Urbanization". The Executive Director of UN-HABITAT, Mrs. Anna Tibaijuka, pointed that, "Reviewing on the sustained growth of cities in the world and the rapid and irreversible urbanization on the planet, we worry not only whether we can manage this growth, but also how we can do it positively so as to make cities into an inclusive, welcoming place for all."

3.2.3 Exploring the Path of China

The 17th National Congress of CPC required to "scientifically analyze the new opportunities and new challenges arising from China's full involvement in economic globalization, fully understand the new situations and new tasks facing China amid the further development of industrialization, informatization, urbanization, marketization, and internationalization, profoundly understand the new issues and new problems faced by China in the future development of the country, conscientiously following the path of scientific development, and arduously strive to open up a broader vista for developing the socialism with Chinese characteristics." Regarding the construction of human settlements, the goal should be demonstrated by two returns to the basics; one is the return to humanism to concern with the lives of the public, and the other is the return to ecological civilization to build human settlements under the guidance of ecological principles.

3.2.3.1　Return to Humanism to Concern with the Lives of the Public

As the core of human settlements is people, the study on human settlements should aim at satisfying the living demands of mankind, which is one of the most fundamental preconditions for the studies of Sciences of Human Settlements [1].

The 17th National Congress of CPC proposed to accelerate the social construction with focus on improving people's livelihood, such as giving priority to education and promoting employment, deepening the reform of income distribution system and increasing the income of urban and rural residents, establishing a social guarantee system that covers both urban and rural residents, completing the medical and health care system and improving the social management, and so on. The public policies of the country are concerned with social justice and social harmony, and advocate building a resources-saving society, livable human settlements, and the multi-leveled housing guarantee system, because they are the basic living demands of mankind.

Housing is an important issue of people's livelihood. Since China's reform and opening-up to the outside world in the 1980s, Chinese cities and towns have seen a rapid development of housing construction, leading to a remarkable improvement of housing of urban residents. Nonetheless, on the other hand, the fact remains that some medium- and low-income families are still in difficulties of housing, which is due to the laggard establishment of a low-rent housing system, the incompletion of an economically affordable housing system, and the imperfection of the corresponding policies and measures. At present, regarding the goals of building a well-off society

---

[1] Wu Liangyong. Introduction to Sciences of Human Settlements. Beijing: China Architecture & Building Press, 2001, pp. 38 – 39.

in an all-round way and establishing a socialist harmonious society, it should become a main public service duty of governments to deal with the housing difficulties of medium- and low-income families, by way of setting up and completing the policy system to focus on the low-rent housing system to solve through multiple channels the problems of housing of low-income families.

With all these basic demands being satisfied, even amid the phantasmagoric changes in the world, China will see the stability of society, the security and healthy of people, the thriving of economy, and the prosperity of culture and technology. Only under such a circumstance, will minds be further opened, science, technology and humanism further innovated, cities and counties further prosper, and people live on the earth poetically and picturesquely.

3.2.3.2 Return to "Ecological Civilization" to Build Human Settlements under the Guidance of Ecological Principles

Aiming at the goal of "building an ecological civilization", the 17th National Congress of CPC required that "the industrial structure, the growth pattern and the consumption mode of energy- and resource-saving and environment-friendliness should be formed. It should promote the large-scale development of recycling economy, considerably increase the proportion of renewable energy resources in total energy consumption, effectively control the discharge of major pollutants, remarkably improve the ecological and environmental quality, and firmly establish the concept of ecological civilization in the whole society." This is not only a practical task of relatively high standard, but also a basic guidance for the development of Sciences of Human Settlements and the construction of human settlements.

Nature has its intrinsic rules governing its development and change, and so does the human society. This kind of intrinsic order of evolution is called law. Only when human society complies with nature and makes use of it, can man survive. Therefore, only by establishing the benign interaction between man and nature and creating harmonious human settlements, can the human society survive and progress. This is the view of ecological civilization of human settlements.

- Nature is the basis of human settlements, from which none of the production activities and construction activities of human settlements can depart.

- Human settlements are the media through which the relationship and the interaction between man and nature take place. The construction of human settlements itself is a form of interaction between man and nature, and the rational construction of human settlements is an integration of the two.

- The construction of human settlements is complicated. In human settlements, people live together to form a society, conduct various social activities, and try to set up livable habitats (buildings) and the supporting networks that are larger in scale and more complicated in contents.

- Man creates human settlements, while human settlements react on man's activities as well [1].

This is why our ancestors emphasized the pursuit of "integrity between man and nature", like SIMA Qian who stressed "exploring the boundary between man and nature, and understanding the changes of past and present", i.e., studying the law of changes between nature and human society. However, this kind of understanding is just the simple view of man and nature.

It has to be mentioned that the ecological civilization is not the mechanical return to nature; instead, it is the adjustment of industrial structure, growth pattern, and consumption mode in line with the principle and mechanism of holistic coordination and recycling. In the practice of about 30 years after China's reform and opening-up to the outside world, we gained a wrong understanding of industrial civilization, believing that we could do whatever we liked with nature, for which we have already reaped the consequences. Today in China, more than 300 million people suffer due to unsafe drinking water, among which 190 million people have to drink water that contains harmful materials beyond the standards; only 66% of the drinking water in the countryside reaches the hygiene standard; above 20 lakes disappear every year, and more than 1,000 inland lakes have vanished since the 1950s [2]. Summing up the

---

[1] WU Liangyong. Introduction to Sciences of Human Settlements. Beijing: China Architecture & Building Press, 2001, pp. 38 – 39.

[2] WANG Shucheng, Minister of Water Resources of the People's Republic of China. Paying Attention to "Rivers and Lakes". Jiefang Weekend, Jan. 4, 2008.

mistakes and lessons of the industrial civilization, we should enter the new era of "ecological civilization", to highlight the environmental consciousness, to preserve the ecological equilibrium, to promote "smart growth", and to achieve harmonious coexistence between man and nature through sustainable development.

In summary, humanism and ecological civilization should be regarded as the basic guidelines for the construction of human settlements. As an issue of value views and moral norms, the core of ecological civilization is "an issue of soul, and the building of ecological civilization is a revolution in the real sense." ❶

3.3 Exploration on and Progress of Theories of Sciences of Human Settlements

The transformation of a development mode brings new requirements to the development of Sciences of Human Settlements. All the innovation systems that can meet the needs of time should be explored with great efforts. This does not mean to develop the Sciences of Human Settlements into a colossal system, nor to simply copy or repeat past experiences, but to improve the different aspects of the Sciences of Human Settlements with regard to the actual problems and in line with the basic principles.

3.3.1 Understanding Human Settlements in a Hierarchical Way

Since the construction system was destroyed in the Culture Revolution and then reestablished in the 1980s, the thought of human settlements has been constantly changing. The Sciences of Human Settlements tries to replace the somewhat abstract concepts like "city" with the unambiguous one of "human settlement", which is more general in terms of both connotation and denotation, in the hope of making the expression more precise. It deals with the entire space on earth, from architectural design at the micro-level, to urban design and environmental design at the medium level, and to urban planning, regional planning, and trans-national spatial planning at the macro-level. Therefore, planning studies at various levels, such as territorial planning, regional planning, urban planning, and town planning, should be strengthened

---

❶ WANG Zhongyu. "Civilization" vs. "Ecology". Science Times, Dec. 3, 2007.

to form the strategic spatial planning system of China, with the scientific ideas of human settlements being fully integrated.

3.3.1.1   From Buildings to Cities [❶]

Based on the experiences of many years, the architectural field has gradually recognized that architecture is not only an issue of building, but also that of city. Therefore, when facing the large-scale urban construction, more and more professionals are devoted to studies on urban design, landscape design, and urban planning.

3.3.1.2   From Cities to Regions

The real urban planning must be regional planning. China's development in the past 30 years proves that the vision of urban planning has been constantly expanding to involve the surroundings of large cities, the metropolitan areas, the city regions, the Yangtze River and Pearl River Delta Regions, the Capital Region of Beijing-Tianjin-Hebei Province, the old industrial base of Northeast China, as well as the river basins (for example, the study on the protection and development of Three Gorges Area, and that on the protection and development of biological and cultural diversity in the area where three rivers go in parallel in the Northwestern Yunnan Province). This is not only the main development tendency but also the new requirements of urban planning. In the past decade, urban planning has been gradually expanded to regional study and regional planning in a conscious way, with the regional studies being widely carried out in the country, including the planning of key development zones and the territorial planning, all of which deepened the concept of region.

However, more efforts should be made to further the development of urban planning to regional study and regional planning, aiming at transforming the common understanding of the academic field into that of the local governments and the whole society. The restrictions on the market in resource allocation should be changed, and the administrative barrier between different regions needs to be broken, so that the achievements of the reform and opening-up can be shared by the entire society.

[❶] WU Liangyong. From City to Region – Science of City and Science of Region. Tianjin: Commission of Coordinated Development of Beijing-Tianjin-Hebei Province. Sept., 1992.

3.3.1.3　From Regions to the World

At present, when the commercial value system and the development mode of the world are undergoing significant changes, it is necessary that a state possesses a considerable power of macro monitoring. While for different regions, it is important to study and draft, based on the independent innovations in accordance with the local conditions, the strategies and tactics that can promote the all-round development of the locality, rather than simply copy the western modes. On the one hand, we should focus on the main tendency of urban development in the world, paying due attention to the studies on large cites, metropolises, city-regions, and world cities, which is now the top concern of the academic field. On the other hand, we need to notice that the studies on the development and construction of rural areas, including the counties, towns, and villages of the fundamental level, are comparatively insufficient.

The necessity to establish a global concept can be interpreted from the following aspects.

(1) With the change in natural conditions like global warming, natural disasters and environmental issues have emerged. Climate change is becoming a complicated issue concerning the global environment, worldwide urban economy, international trade, etc., as well as a common threat that mankind is facing. The rise in sea level and its countermeasures are another big issue. In the coastal areas of China, the speed of sea level rise is higher than the average of the world, with that of Tianjin being the highest and Shanghai the second. This deserves due attention of the Chinese Government. [1] The improvement of environment is an important part of development, whose urgency should be fully recognized along with the frequent occurrence of natural disasters.

(2) The progress of various technologies like transportation and information brings about the phenomena of "time-space concentration", which influences not only the development of politics, economy, and society of the world, but also the transformation of regional development mode. For instance, the mode of "separating while interconnecting" put forward by the author of "Europe: A History for the

---

[1] In the coastal area of China, the sea level has risen by 90 mm in the past 30 years, with the sea level rise in Tianjin of 196 mm being the fastest, and that in Shanghai of 115 mm being the second. In 2007, the sea level rise in China was 2.5 mm, which was higher than the average of the world of 1.8 mm. Official Report on China Marine Environment Quality 2007.

European development" can be also suitable for global development.[1] Meanwhile, China should use as a reference the practice of the European Union in spatial planning [2].

(3) Amid economic globalization, the collaborations and competitions based on national interests should be reviewed in a holistic way from a global perspective. Neither the transformations of city and society, nor the changes of space and time concepts can be dealt without the background of globalization.

In the 1980s, John Friedmann put forward the concept of "World City", while a decade later, Sassen brought forth the concept of "Global City", both of which can help us understand how the forces influence the development of specific cities. It should be noticed that international factors are playing a more and more significant role on local issues, making the localities face the influences of globalization. For example, international investment is becoming more and more important, the flow of production factors in the world are becoming stronger and stronger, the technical supports and knowledge-based industries are dominating in the social affairs, and the scaled market is playing a central role.

3.3.1.4　Coordination of City and Countryside

Supplementary to each other, city and countryside are the premise of one another's existence, which should not be dissevered by man. In the past, planning work used to be limited to cities and rural settlements, with quite few holistic studies. Restricted by the dual economic structure, the rural development in China has lagged behind for a long time, and many problems are hard to be solved for the time being.

The theme of World Habitat Day of the United Nations in 2004 was "Cities – Engines of Rural Development". Anna Tibaijuka, Executive Director of UN-HABITAT, appealed in a letter to people in all walks of life that the urban-rural issue should be treated in a holistic way. "In order to keep the sustainability of both urban and rural development, the interdependence between each other should be better straightened out, and more effective administration be exercised. The urgent problem that we

---

[1] N. Davies. Europe: A History.

[2] HUO Bing. Strategic Spatial Planning: Theory and Practice in China. Doctor degree dissertation of Tsinghua University, 2006.

are facing currently is that the urban development fails to promote the agriculture, and the improvement of regional productivity neither makes any progress in the infrastructures. [1]"

In spite of the strategic guidelines of "industry feeding back agriculture" and "city supporting countryside", China's countryside is still facing many urgent problems that call for due attention and effective solutions, such as how to balance rural development with urban development, how to explore the way of rural urbanization, how to relocate the millions of rural population in cities and transfer them into urban population, how to promote effective village development in the developed areas, and how to deal with environment issues in the countryside (for example, environmental pollution caused by coal burning for household life, the over-use of fertilizers, and the disordered development of township enterprises, the security of drinking water, and so on). The construction of "New Socialist Countryside" has enormous creation scope in the vast rural area that accounts for three-fourth of the entire territory of China. It involves not only the issues of improving personal quality, popularizing preliminary education and health care, and ameliorating physical environment, but also those of fostering and developing the "county economy", which is characterized by modern agriculture and local industry, renovating with high technologies the traditional industries that should not be completely abandoned, and protecting the ecological environment and cultural heritages. The rural construction in the vast central and western China would even lead to the emergence of the specific modernization pattern of China.

Rural development is always the basis for the socio-economic development of China. During the historic evolution of over 2,000 years from the Qin and Han Dynasties to the 1950s, "county" had been the basic administrative unit of the agricultural society of China, keeping relatively stable for a long time as the economic basis for the feudal regimes. After the foundation of the People's Republic of China, "county" was still an important administrative unit of local level. Currently in China, there are about 2,010 county-level administrative units (including county-level cities) and 35,000 towns and villages. Since 2002, the Central Government of China has advocated several times "promoting county economy". A county is an economic system, as well as a social and cultural one. It can

---

[1] Anna K. Telajiaka. May 25, 2004.

be also regarded as the basic planning unit that integrates territorial planning, regional planning, and urban planning. This is one of the most fundamental countermeasures to deal with globalization that is full of uncertain factors.

3.3.2　Problem-Oriented Multidisciplinary Integration

3.3.2.1　Integrating Architecture, City Planning, Landscape Architecture, and Science and Technology for Holistic Creation

The concept of physical environment construction [1] was introduced to China in the second half of the 1940s, referring to the harmonious and orderly development of the planning, construction, and administration of the substantial physical environment that ranges from furniture and house to city and region, and from the art of urban and rural construction to that of landscape and gardening.

Architecture, city planning, landscape architecture and science and technology that take the physical environment as main study object should be integrated for holistic creation. This is the preliminary requirement of the Sciences of Human Settlements. As early as 1996, I had proposed the idea of integrating architecture, landscape architecture, and city planning [2] in view of their commonness in the following aspects:

- The same goal of creating livable human settlements with humanistic concerns;

- The same pursuit for the amenity of physical environment, the soundness of ecology, and the return to nature;

- The same concerns about land-use and the protection of natural and cultural resources;

- The same feature of the creation of art, science, and technology; and

- The same basis of engineering.

What is more important is that, nowadays, the exploration and the construction of eco-building, eco-city, and eco-environment require integrating the man-made environment with the natural environment by more comprehensive means.

Actually, the mutual cross-link, infiltration and complement of these three

---

[1] This concept was introduced to China by Prof. LIANG Sicheng in 1947 when he returned from his lectures in the United States.

[2] WU Liangyong. Future of Architecutre. Beijing, Tsinghua University Press, 2002; and WU Liangyong, UIA Beijing Charter, Beijing: Tsinghua University Press, 2002.

disciplines for comprehensive innovation form the core of the Sciences of Human Settlements. One may wonder why they developed into separate disciplines. The reason is that they were developed respectively in Europe and North America along with the process of urbanization and based on different historic background and market context. Conforming to the tradition of industrial association each formed the schools and organization of its own without willing to follow others blindly. But why do we emphasize their integration in China? The reason lies in the facts of accelerating urbanization and large-scale construction that make almost every project involve several aspects of socio-economic development. This is why due attention was paid to their integration in the past two decades particularly in the academic and educational fields of architecture.

The following points are also elucidated in the Beijing Charter of the International Union of Architects, which was approved in 1999:

(1) To regard the construction, utilization, operation, renovation, and renewal of a building as a cycling system, and to strengthen the reutilization, renovation, expansion, and rehabilitation of buildings in urban renewal, rather than to destroy them on a large scale for satisfying the operational needs of real estate;

(2) To structure a multi-leveled technical system;

(3) To establish the "glo-cal architecture" on the basis of cultural diversity;

(4) To highlight the integrity of environmental art; and

(5) To advocate architecture for all [1].

3.3.2.2　Carrying out Problem-Oriented and Multidisciplinary Studies

As the world is always changing, it is impossible for architects, planners, and other professionals to determine how and where the human society will go. However, they could make use of new technologies to create a livable environment for public according to the development of the times and the requirements of the society. For this, they must keep seeking new ideas and countermeasures, not only to integrate architecture, city planning, landscape architecture, and science and technology for holistic creation, but also to integrate the research outcomes concerning human

---

[1] WU Liangyong. Future of Architecutre. Beijing: Tsinghua University Press, 2002.

settlements in the fields of geography, ecology, environment, and economics to deal with the problems and challenges of spatial development that man is facing today.

In view of the resource shortage in today's world, economic growth must be coordinated with the development of environment, resources, and society by adopting the strategies of green development, energy saving, and emission reduction. This holds good for urban construction too. With the development of transport technologies, the reduction of space distance, and the utilization of underground space, the time-space concept of human settlements will be changed. Therefore, pedestrian travel should be restricted, automobile use be restricted, public transport be preferential, and transport technologies be diversified. We need to structure a reasonable spatial pattern for cities and regions by using the idea of "compact city". Moreover, the new technologies of geographic information system will surely promote the development of the sciences to a great extent if they can be effectively applied and popularized.

Only when it can deal with the practical problems, can the Sciences of Human Settlements be developed; for instance, how to save energy and land resources, how to deal with the dilemma of urban sprawl and land waste, how to handle the proportions of social housing development and commercial housing development, etc. None of these problems is simply a technical one. Owing to the lack of public spirit and the pursuit of "maximal profits", science and technology are distorted to a certain degree, making the real technological creativity unable to function normally. In fact, the resolution to these intractable problems lies in the integration of science, technology, and humanism, the improvement of physical environment, and the building of political civilization. This is why our exploration on human settlements has been expanded, within the field of physical environment, from the issues limited to buildings to those concerning multi-leveled spatial pattern to advocate strategic spatial planning, and even further to the fields of sociology and culture to promote the construction of a cultural city. It can be concluded that the Sciences of Human Settlements advocates the combination of science and humanism, letting science promote the reforms on the construction of human settlements, while humanism guides the development of science.

It should be stated that the Sciences of Human Settlements is not a single discipline of a colossal and rigid academic system, but a group of disciplines that are integrated together based on the requirements of the era for solving practical problems. As an academic system of an organic, open, and growing disciplinary set, it can be expanded and innovated during the problem-solving process.

3.3.3 Inheritance and Innovation of the Culture of Human Settlement

Culture is the total of physical and spiritual wealth. The improvement of human settlements refers to not only the promotion of physical wealth, but also the creation of residential culture and cultural environment.

3.3.3.1 Absorbing the Essence of Chinese Culture and Carrying out Comprehensive Innovation

The development of Sciences of Human Settlements relies on the accumulation of spiritual culture, which gives off the sparkle of creation in different aspects. In the splendid Chinese culture, the culture of human settlement is a brilliant part. For example, in terms of architecture, China sees a diversified and distinctive architectural system due to the integration of Chinese culture with foreign cultures, local culture, and ethnic cultures.

Even when Chinese emperors began to decline in the early stage of China's modernization at the turn of 19th century, there appeared SUN Yat-sen's "General Plan for National Development", which is equivalent to today's national territorial planning, and ZHANG Jian's idea of "regional and local construction" and his great practice in Nantong that is boasted of as an "ideal cultural city", both of which make Chinese people have every reason to be proud of the brilliant culture of human settlement.

Today, when China enjoys great prosperity and progress in the 21st Century and foreign sciences, technologies, and cultures swarm into China with rich inspirations, we should be more confident of the wisdom of Chinese culture and take it as our responsibility to carry forward the Chinese culture and to carry out independent innovations, so as to create the distinct features of the new era in the process of building a socialism rich in Chinese characteristics.

3.3.3.2　Active Protection and Holistic Creation

It can be concluded from the above analysis that the history of human settlement is actually that of human settlement civilization. As the congregation of different aspects, it evolved along with the political, economic, social, and cultural changes of the era, full of disparities and conflicts as well as communications and integrations. It kept growing and upgrading with endless progress.

Nowadays, both historic areas and the scenic areas are destroyed to a great extent by the popularization of "dominant culture", the mediocre commercial development, the excessive tourism development, and the large-scale real estate operation that come along with globalization. With regard to this cultural phenomenon, positive protection cannot block or resist the torrent of destruction. Cultural mediocrity can in turn affect the economic development. For instance, regarding the historic and cultural cities, the great efforts of protecting the historic buildings cannot counteract the large-scale destruction of the mediocre new buildings. On the contrary, it should integrate the protection of the old with the construction of the new to establish a new order of development. This refers to setting up a "buffer area" surrounding the cultural heritages, where the architectural style of originality and conformability with the traditional buildings should be advocated, and to vigorously carry out "active protection and holistic creation" in line with local cultures and with high-quality skills, so as to create a diversified urban culture and to shape a new urban environment characterized by both time spirit and traditional feature.

3.3.3.3　Urban Culture as an Important Research Project of the Sciences of Human Settlements

China has seen remarkable socio-economic development and accelerated urbanization since its reform and opening-up to the world. At the same time, it has to face complicated cultural problems that are closely related to the important social phenomena such as modernization, economic globalization, and sustainable development.

The revival of Chinese people will definitely be accompanied by the prosperity of Chinese culture. Today, culture is more and more becoming an important source for national solidarity and creativity, a vital factor in the competitiveness of a country, and a keen wish of the public to enrich their spiritual and cultural life. Therefore, the research on urban culture should highlight the culture of human settlement, local culture, eco-culture, innovative culture, and so on, so as to boost the development of cultural and innovative industries, to promote the harmonious development between culture and city, and to facilitate the growth of innovative cities.

Yet, how to recognize the spiritual value of urban culture from the strategic perspective to build cities with soul? How to creatively and effectively utilize the cultural resources to explore the path of sustainable development for China's urbanization? How to exert the important role of culture in the construction of urban innovation environment to improve the content and quality of urban culture? How to formulate the comprehensive and integral cultural policies to actively respond to the trend of cultural commercialization? How to conduct cultural planning to demonstrate the social justice in the construction of cityscape? In view of all these problems to be solved, urban culture will undoubtedly become a main research project of the Sciences of Human Settlements [1].

3.4 Methodology and Action Guide

3.4.1 Appreciation on Methodology

JIN Wulun once pointed out that the key methodology of the Sciences of Human Settlements is holism, which is a distinctive methodology that integrates the essence of traditional Chinese culture and the achievements of contemporary sciences, i.e. , the Science of Complexity. Even the dialectical unification of reductionism and holism is actually the pursuit for integrity, which can be regarded as a "growing whole" [2].

Based on the multidisciplinary integration, the holism of the Sciences of Human

---

[1] WU Tinghai. Present and Prospect of Study on Urban Culture. Report on Progress of Urban Studies (2007 – 2008). Chinese Society for Urban Studies, 2008.

[2] JIN Wulun's lecture in the course of Intorduction to Sceinces of Human Settlements at Tsinghua University. C. Alexander also put forward the concept of "growing whole" based on his analyses on the development phases of Rome.

Settlements is aimed at seeking solutions to the actual problems. This is why the planning of different levels must be based on an innovative knowledge system.

Planning and construction is a process. In view of the different conditions of different areas and the various uncertainties in the development process, there are always many possibilities of development for a locality. Therefore for decision-making, different schemes should be listed and compared, so as to select the scheme for the first-phased construction following the principle of more advantageous achievements with the completion of the construction and less disadvantageous influences on future development. After the implementation of the first-phased scheme, new changes may happen to the existing conditions. Thus, the original overall scheme should be revised accordingly. The cycle of implementation and revision runs through the whole process of development.

Planning is usually based on numerous investigations and researches. This kind of work is quite necessary as long as it is scientific and reasonable, particularly to avoid the waste of time and energy and the irrational choice that may cause hidden troubles in future development.

Human knowledge of the world at the very beginning is of simple holism. However, along with the development of human society, especially the rapid development of commercial society and the accelerated development of science and technology since the Industrial Revolution, the pursuit for maximal individual or departmental interest brought about the overall deterioration of the environment, the decline of the concept of holistic interest, and the ignorance of entirety. We have to reconsider this issue when it becomes a threat to the environment, resources, and even the destiny of humankind, for which, it will inevitably be our attitude to return to holism to critically integrate and to organically deal with the relationships between different aspects by adopting the concept of "growing whole."

In fact, the scientific view of development reveals the transformation of the development mode in China. We should discover the inadaptability of human settlements to the requirements of the society from different perspectives, and explore new development modes in different aspects. For this, due efforts should be made to coordinate various aspects, in terms of not only concrete action but also ideological guideline. Ideological guidelines refer to the changes in development concepts and philosophical ideas, as well as the recognition of and re-exploration on a cultural basis; concrete action refers to taking technical and humanistic measures in line with the specific conditions of locality and times to ensure the coordination of various aspects.

3.4.2   Action Guide

The Sciences of Human Settlement is not merely an academic concept or a theoretical framework. It also helps conduct researches, guide practices, and take actions. Planning is a collective behavior of human society, whose paradigm evolves with the changes of socio-economic development. New things have been constantly emerging along with the evolution of social thoughts. For instance, in the late 19th Century, the planning theories in the west were divided into four categories, i.e., social reform, policy analysis, social learning, and social mobilization [1]. In China, urban planning was first established in the 1950s, and experienced its revitalization after China's reform and opening-up. The promulgation of the Urban and Rural Planning Law of the People's Republic of China that took effect in 2008 is another significant event in the history of urban and rural construction of China. It states the significance of balanced urban and rural planning, which is an indispensable measure to implement the theories of social reform, social learning, and social mobilization, as well as the strategic tactic to carry out the policy of accelerating the social construction with focus on improving people's livelihood that was put forward in the 17th National Congress of CPC.

3.4.3   Gathering the Wisdom of the Whole Society to Develop the Sciences of Human Settlements

Human settlements concern every aspect of the life of each household. When they are built in good order to make people live and work in peace and contentment, the whole society will be stable, prosperous, and peaceful. However, once a major accident

---

[1] J. Friedmann. Planning in the Public Domain. 1987.

happens, whether it is a natural disaster or a disaster caused by human activities, it will inevitably affect people's daily life to a great extent, and even disturb the order of the country and the society, and hinder the completion of major tasks. For building better human settlements, the following should be highlighted.

Firstly, intellectuals should transform the professional contents of the different disciplines that the Sciences of Human Settlements concern into general knowledge that can be easily understood and accepted by the public, and make them into the common goals of the whole society. They should share every weal and woe with the people and spare no effort to mobilize the whole society for achieving the goals.

Secondly, the construction of livable environment is a collective creation of all the citizens. We should trust the public and believe in their creativity. Even though cities and towns are a complicated system and the growing whole of self-organization, and new matters keep emerging with time, we should believe that the public contains the great potential of creation to deal with all the new problems. Thus, efforts should be made to develop community awareness, arouse environmental concern, and inspire the self-perfection ability of the citizens, so as to build a "close environment", "livable environment", and "livable community". As long as we care for the society, it is easy to find that the citizens are more and more concerned with the public benefits, for example, the active participation of the citizens of Beijing in the protection of the Old Summer Palace and the renovation of Shichahai Area. To achieve sustained development, a city must concern the life of its citizens and be managed by diversified measures. There is an occidental saying that "citizens build cities." In China, there is a similar one that "the city of people should be built by the people and serve the people". We should develop the pattern of social governance characterized by "social collaboration and public participation". The construction of livable cities involves the improvement of life quality, the completion of housing guarantee system, the establishment of index system, the promotion of public administration, the realization of social justice, etc.

Thirdly, the construction of livable cities is also the compelling obligation of local governments. The diversified historic cities of China are actually the result of the collective creation and management of workers, poets, scholars, citizens, and upright officials of generations in the long history of several dynasties. For instance, in Hangzhou, BAI Juyi, the famous poet of the Tang Dynasty, wrote the tender poem of "reserving the lake **❶** for you to live on in famine years' before quitting his official post; SU Dongpo, the well-known poet of the Song Dynasty, strived against the despots to protect the West Lake and submitted twice a written statement to the higher authorities for dredging up the lake. In Shaoxing, MA Zhen, the mayor of the city in the Han Dynasty, even sacrificed his life for renovating the Jian Lake. The builders of generations in history not only improved the natural environment to make it more livable, but also created a pleasant man-made environment with rich imaginations in a scientific and artistic way. The development of these historic cities has proved that a city can be built according to the governors" ambitions, but what is more important is that it must be built on the basis of scientific planning. Moreover, as cannot be mentioned in the same breath, today's city is much more complicated than that of the agricultural society. Therefore, it is unpardonable for government officials, especially the decision-makers of a city, to make wrong or even irrevocable decisions due to the lack of scientific knowledge and humanistic breeding and the limitation of departmental or local interest.

There is a Chinese proverb saying that "there have been lots of poets out of prefects since ancient times". It is not easy for a decision-maker to be good at writing poems; however, it is more important for him to notice the complication of the matters that human settlements concern. In view of significance and difficulty, the construction of human settlements exceeds all kinds of civil projects of general sense. Therefore, the decision-makers should be farsighted in theory and skillful in practice. For the cause of improving human settlements for millions of people, they should adhere to lofty ideals, surefooted in performing the duties, and well equipped with the scientific attitude of realism and the comprehensive ability of strategic tactics, for example, to mobilize the

---

❶ Editor's note: The lake here refers to the West Lake.

initiatives of experts to solve the actual problems, to encourage the public to care for their own homes, and to devote themselves to the construction of their homeland. Only those decision-makers with considerable knowledge on the humanism of the city and its region and the ability to realize social ideals can be regarded as qualified.

Fourthly, efforts should be made to ameliorate the social environment. A better human settlement relies on not only a sound physical environment, but also a healthy and harmonious social environment. The following should be advocated: creating good social atmosphere, setting up high ethical standards, respecting nature, treasuring "material resources", and utilizing and saving the resources, so as to ensure a sustainable development of society.

The Sciences of Human Settlements is at the frontier of science, but it deserves further development and calls for more knowledge. This is the truth for intellectuals, the society, and the decision-makers as well. We are looking forward to reaching a common understanding firstly in scientific fields, then in the whole society, and finally in the process of decision-making, so as to gradually develop the Sciences of Human Settlements to a new realm. The development of Sciences of Human Settlements is an indispensable content of social reform, for which we can borrow the remark of ZHANG Zai of the Song Dynasty to express our lofty sentiments and aspirations: "pursue the law of nature, explore the way of living for the people, inherit the achievements of the ancient sages, and create the peace for all ages!"

Author's note: This paper contains the closing remarks that I made on December 25, 2007 in the course of Introduction to Sciences of Human Settlements at School of Architecture, Tsinghua University. In 1996, I wrote with strong emotions a paper titled "From Songlinpo of Chongqing to Istanbul", as the postscript for the book "Toward the Future of New Century: Paper Collection of Urban Studies of WU Liangyong". Today, as China's socio-economic development is entering a new stage, I am trying to reconsider the new situation faced by planning and construction in this paper.

On Wu Liangyong's Theories about Sciences of Human Settlements

By WU Tinghai

A.1   Introduction

Human settlement is a comprehensive frontier science first proposed in the world during the second half of the 20th Century and has been gradually developed till this day. It studies countryside, cities, and all other human settlement environments, focusing on the relationship between people and environment, emphasizing the integrity of human settlement, and adopting a systematic and comprehensive approach studying all aspects including politics, society, culture, and technology. Wu Liangyong is the founder of human settlement science in China. Facing the complexity and integration or urban and rural construction in China, on the basis of existing studies of human settlement, he constructed in a creative way the theoretical system, academic framework, and methodology of the science of human settlement in China, making them basic theories guiding urban and rural planning and construction in this country. He sticks to the life philosophy of "reading as many books as possible, traveling to as many places as possible, acknowledging as many people as possible as teachers, and managing to provide housing to as many people as possible", and works hard for realizing a harmonious society and a beautiful construction environment till this day. This article mainly discusses his academic theories on human settlement, centering on three fields of their formation, features, as well as research methodology.

A.2   Formation of Human Settlement Theories

In his "Introduction to Human Settlement Science" published in 2002, Wu Liangyong reviewed briefly the formation process of his theories on human settlement based on his personal experience, according to which I roughly divide the process into three stages of budding (before 1985), taking shape (1985-2002), and blossoming (after 2003).

A.2.1   The Stage of Budding (before 1985)

It has been over 60 years since Wu Liangyong came to teach at Tsinghua University in 1946. He divided his work experience into two parts with the dividing line of year 1985: (1) before 1985 and during 1946-1966, with a passion for work, he mainly engaged in daily and routine department operation, and managed to restore during 1978-1984 the Department of Architecture which was greatly damaged during the Great Cultural Revolution; (2) after 1985, he founded and was in charge of Institute of Architecture & Urban Studies, Tsinghua University[1]. In view of the formation of theories on human settlement, it's the stage of budding (or preparation) before 1985, forming such theories on living and housing, on spatial environment, and on comprehensive development of multiple disciplines.

A.2.1.1　Theories on Living and Housing

Living and housing are important concepts of human settlement and serve as one of the sources of theories on human settlement proposed by Wu Liangyong.

(1) All people shall have a place to live in

Wu Liangyong was born in Menxi, Nanjing, in 1922, a place adjacent to the famous Qinhuai River, which used to be a flourishing area well known for culture, business, services, and professional processing industry before declining greatly shortly after the Republic of China (1912-1949) was founded. Spending his childhood in such a place, Wu Liangyong and his family had to leave the hometown, becoming displaced and suffering a great deal. Shortly before the city of Nanjing was seized by Japanese army in 1937, Wu Liangyong left Nanjing in a hurry along with his elder brother. Witnessing the land falling into enemy hands, being homeless, and experiencing a hard life, Wu Liangyong made up his mind to reconstruct the hometown someday. Therefore, he went to National Central University in 1940 and studied architecture, receiving scientific education on "providing housing for all", expecting the great reconstruction projects after the war.

(2) The concept of living in a broad sense and in a narrow sense

Wu Liangyong recalled that the first lesson he learned at Tsinghua University in 1946 was "three principles of architecture: the concept of living in a broad sense and in a narrow sense[2] a concept originating from the lessons on ancient architecture taught

---

[1] Wu Liangyong, "History of Institute of Architecture & Urban Studies, Tsinghua University", Tianjin, 9 January 2006.

[2] Wu Liangyong, "Fifty Years at School of Architecture, Tsinghua University", Collection in Commemoration of the 50th Anniversary of School (Department) of Architecture, Tsinghua University, ed. by Zhao Bingshi and Chen Yanqing, China Architecture and Building Press, 1996.

by Bao Ding and being adopted by Wu Liangyong in modern education of architecture, which further develop the concept of living in a narrow sense. Accordingly, another concept of architecture in a broad sense was created, such as Tsinghua Garden and Beijing City, which served as the foundation for integrating architecture with surrounding external environment.

(3) Housing, Environment, Urban, and Rural Construction

In 1983, CAS Department of Science and Technology planned to hold an academic seminar in Changchun. Wu Liangyong, Zhou Ganzhi, and Lin Zhiqun jointly drafted for Architecture Division a report, "Housing, Environment, Urban, and Rural Construction", which pointed out on a timely basis many important issues of population, housing, public facilities, land, and environment concerning architectural development in China at that time before proposing relevant strategic countermeasures and recommendations. In fact, they have consciously integrated housing with the environment and urban and rural construction, which then gradually developed into theories on human settlement.

A.2.1.2　Theories on Spatial Environment

Theories on spatial environment serve another important source for Wu Liangyong to form his theories on human settlement.

(1) Inheriting the Theories on Physical Environment proposed by Liang Sicheng

In 1947, Liang Sicheng returned to China from his investigation tour on US education in architecture and felt that both European and US architecture communities emphasized city planning, "constructing well-organized and orderly new cities so as to create complete and healthy physical environment for people," [1] which China should learn for construction projects after the war. The most fundamental objective of new modern architectural theories is "to create a physical environment in favor of physical and mental health of mankind for both living and working." The concept of "physical environment" refers to concrete environment covering extensively small objects such as a light, an ink stone, a cup and a saucer,

---

[1] Liang Sicheng, "Telegram Drafted on Behalf of Mei Yiqi for the Ministry of Education", 1948, Tsinghua University Archives, Complete Works by Liang Sicheng (Vol. 5), China Architecture and Building Press, 2001.

and large objects such as a city, as well as the connections among different cities in a region, and reasonable and appropriate "stages" constructed for living and working in such fields of culture, politics, industries, and business; all these are the objects of physical environment planning. The curriculum arrangement of Department of Architecture, Tsinghua University, also reflected the philosophy of designing physical environment in a broad sense. [1]

Wu Liangyong (2001b) believes that Liang Sicheng developed the concept of general architecture into the concept of physical environment, "although his theories still emphasize aesthetics, yet have already focused on integrated environment." Due to the changes of the time and the rapid progress of urbanization in China, construction projects have been launched on a large scale and at high speed in both urban and rural areas, and the tasks and content of architecture have greatly expanded on the basis of traditional concept of architecture, requiring a theoretical framework for the development of architecture in a larger scope and at a higher level. Wu Liangyong believes that what he has done "is to continue the unfinished work started by Mr. Liang Sicheng," [2] and is the further development in the field.

(2) Summarizing Traditional Chinese Theories on Spatial Environment

In 1984, the architecture community in mainland China actively prepared for the Lanting Conference jointly held with their counterparts in Taiwan, and the theme was "Traditional Concept of Environment and Modern Environment Designing". The conference was not held due to certain reasons, but Wu Liangyong finished his paper on the creation of environment in the history and traditional concept of environment in China, in which he argues that one of the main features of traditional Chinese environmental designing is a holistic view, including multi-leveled spatial perspective, measurement perspective for different levels, artistic perspective of basic spatial unit, while all the perspectives of environment development, culture, nature, and integration are co-related and unified, jointly forming the theories on designing and creating environment (Wu Liangyong, 1985).

---

[1] Liang Sicheng, "Draft Plan on Educational System and Curriculum of Department of Architecture", Wenhui Daily, 10-12 July 1949, Complete Works by Liang Sicheng (Vol. 5), China Architecture and Building Press, 2001.

[2] Wu Liangyong, "What I Found When I Look back the Past 80 Years", the speech delivered at Seminar on Architecture and City Development during the 21st Century, April 27, 2004.

A.2.1.3   Comprehensive Multi-Disciplinary Studies

Comprehensive multi-disciplinary studies serve as the foundation for methodology of studying human settlement science. At the meeting announcing the founding of Chinese Society for Urban Studies held in January 1984, Wu Liangyong made a speech entitled "Comprehensive Multi-Disciplinary Development: An Inevitable Road for Urban Studies". ❶ He studied the development trend of multi-disciplinary studies in the history of modern urban studies in the west as well as the development of the studies in China through urban construction practice, proposing to actively promote the comprehensive multi-disciplinary approach in urban studies. When many scholars and experts had the feeling that the studies and knowledge on cities should not be restricted to city planning and construction but should further expand the scope and vision of studies, Wu Liangyong proposed at the meeting to launch urban studies, which was a great breakthrough in architecture community at that time in view of ideological liberation and promotion of tradition (Chen, Weibang, 2002).

At the academic meeting held by the Department of Architecture, Tsinghua University, in May 1984, Wu Liangyong delivered a speech, "The Development of City Planning Studies and The Education of Architecture", emphasizing the merging and integration of multiple disciplines and that the Department of Architecture would develop the science of human habitat environment, which is probably the first time that Wu Liangyong proposed the "science of human settlements" from a multi-disciplinary perspective. He believed that it was "a new and comprehensive discipline, requiring the integration of multiple disciplinary results so as to better construct our living environment"(Wu Liangyong, 1984a).

Being sponsored by a scientific fund granted by the State Education Committee and during 1983-1985, Wu Liangyong was in charge of the research project titled "Comparative Studies on Chinese City Structures and Forms", making clear the research methodology of comprehensive multi-disciplinary studies on the relationship between city structure and form, which lays a solid foundation for future research on

---

❶ Wu Liangyong, "Comprehensive Multi-Disciplinary Development: An Inevitable Road for Urban Studies", Urban Studies in China (Vol. 1), 1984.

urban and regional space.

To sum up, through years of personal experience, study, research, and practice before 1985, Wu Liangyong gradually formed his theories on living and spatial environment and the research methodology of comprehensive multi-disciplinary studies, which serve as the basic conditions for the formation of his theories on human settlement.

A.2.2　The Stage of Taking Shape (1985-2002)

After 1985, China adopted policies of reform and opening-up. Both the economy and society have grown rapidly, and urban and rural construction have gradually been regulated. However, at the same time, there have occurred a lot of complicated problems, which has been the general background for theories on human settlement coming into being.

A.2.2.1　"General Theory of Architecture and Theories on Settlement" (1987-1989)

In 1981, Wu Liangyong came back from West Germany where he had been a lecturer and found through comparing Chinese and foreign architectural development that it is hard for Chinese architecture to be extensively understood and accepted or to further develop without promoting it to a higher level as a science. In order to make architecture a science, there should be comprehensive research requirements, as well as "a comprehensive understanding on the undertaking of architecture so as to have an integrated and complete understanding on buildings". He therefore advocated studying architecture by integrating other main elements. After years of preparation, the Seminar on Future of Architecture Science was finally held in Tsinghua University on August 19, 1987, during which Wu Liangyong proposed the concept of "general architecture" for the first time. "A General Theory of Architecture" by Wu Liangyong was published in September 1989, and according to his theories on settlements, architecture develops from the simple concept of "shelter" to the concept of "settlement", which is the concept covering much bigger scope of one building, a village of three families, a town, a city, a big city, and even a mega city, "focusing on the construction of human habitat environment" (Wu Liangyong, 1990a). Accordingly, architecture integrates with cities as well as the studies of sociology and anthropology, which greatly promotes the complete understanding on human architectural activities (Wu Liangyong, 1989).

The theory of settlement is a basic theory, starting from which will make one gain a better understanding of regional, cultural, and technological features of architecture, leading finally to the "general architecture". With the help of settlement theories, Wu Liangyong managed to integrate his previous research fruits of "living in a broad sense", "spatial environment", and "comprehensive multi-disciplinary studies" and created the initial theories on human settlement.

In order to celebrate the World Architecture Festival (July 1), the Architectural Society of China held on June 27, 1990 a seminar on Human Settlement, during which Wu Liangyong delivered a keynote speech, "Creating New Landscape of Human Settlement in China". He pointed out that human settlement is a common problem facing the entire world, but we always work under specific conditions in a specific country with specific social, economic, technological features, different productivity levels, and under different traditions; in other words, we always work in specific time and spatial conditions, create with specific conditions, solve different problems in different ways, choose different paths of development, and have different ways in handling conflicts and difficulties. The theory of general architecture is an attempt to focus on the new scenarios in China. Deputy Minister Tan Qinglian of Construction also made a speech at the seminar, "Dedicating to the Great Career of Improving Human Settlement Environment" (Tan Qinglian, 1990). The Academic Committee of Human Settlements, Institute of Architects, Architectural Society of China, was founded shortly after the seminar.

A.2.2.2   Proposal of "Science of Human Settlements" (1993)

CAS Department of Science and Technology held an Academy Members Reporting Meeting on August 4, 1993, during which Wu Liangyong, Zhou Ganzhi, and Lin Zhiqun reported on their studies with the theme of "Today and Tomorrow of China Construction Industry: Prospect of Human Settlement Science". In view of the conflicts and problems that occurred during the unprecedented progress of urban and rural development in China in the 1980s, the report proposed a new academic concept and systematic theories on the science of human settlement. This is a science studying the protection and development of architectural as well as urban man-made and natural environment on the basis of human production and living activities (Wu Liangyong, Zhou Ganzhi, Lin Zhiqun, 1994; CAS Department of Science and Technology, 1994). Accordingly, it develops from a unitary subject to a comprehensive science in a broad sense, creating a new disciplinary system integrating all subjects concerning the creation and development of human habitat environment (including natural sciences, technological sciences, and human sciences). This is the first time that the theories on science of human settlement were officially proposed. This academic report and the report on Housing, Environment, Urban, and Rural Construction composed in 1983 were published under the title "Today and Tomorrow of China Construction Industry".

The authorities attached significant importance to the science of human settlements. On August 23, 1993, China Science and Technology News published a front page story, "Prospect of Architecture in China: Academy Member Wu Liangyong on Science of Human Settlements". On November 12, 1994, the National Natural Science Foundation of China held in Kunming the Seminar on Human Settlement Environment and Chinese Architecture in the 21st Century, during which Wu Liangyong delivered the keynote speech, "Developing Human Settlement Science Facing the New Century". He pointed out that the construction of human settlements initiated the birth of a new subject, the science of human settlements, which is a new disciplinary system studying the protection and development of architectural as well as urban man-made and natural environment on the basis of human production and living activities (Wu Liangyong, 1995).

A.2.2.3   The Founding of Center for Human Settlements, Tsinghua University (1995)

With the impact of "Today and Tomorrow of China Construction Industry", Tsinghua University Carder Meeting (or Sanbao Meeting) started to prepare the founding of the Center for Human Settlements. In order to better organize and launch scientific studies on human settlement, Tsinghua University founded the Center for Human Settlements on November 28, 1995, involving six departments and schools, namely, School of Architecture, Civil Engineering Department, Department of Hydraulic Engineering, Department of Environmental Engineering, Thermal Engineering Department, and School of Economics and Management. Wu Liangyong served as the director of the Center. During the opening ceremony, Wu Liangyong made a speech and elaborated the development background, research content, content, strategy, and organization of the science of human settlements, pointing out that the Center for Human Settlements is an organization focusing on the studies of issues concerning human settlements and that it is a growing academic community, covering all relevant departments, institutes, and majors at the university. The purpose of establishing human settlement science, however, is to develop it from a unitary subject to a comprehensive discipline in the broad sense instead of replacing or overtopping existing subjects with the science of human settlements (Wu Liangyong, 1996b). Then, Wu Liangyong held and organized a series of lectures introducing the science of human settlements at Tsinghua University. Many other schools and colleges also set up academic courses on the science of human settlements, which have gradually and steadily gained support and emphasis.

A.2.2.4　The NSFC Sponsors a Series of Theoretical Studies and Academic Discussions on Human Settlement (1993-2000)

From 1993 to 1997, the National Natural Science Foundation of China (NSFC) sponsored Wu Liangyong to organize "Studies on the Protection and Development of Architectural Environment in Developed Areas during Urbanization Progress" (a key project during the 8th Five-Year-Plan). In February 1993, Wu Liangyong pointed out in a dissertation proposal that in a system composed of nature, space, and people, in order to construct regional human settlement including regional transport network, urban network, urban and rural integrated pattern, and open spatial system, we should: (1) look for dynamic and complicated forms; (2) create integrated and harmonious beauty out of chaos; (3) look for visual forms in multifarious large city areas, managing to achieve harmonious areas integrating manpower with nature and urban area with rural areas, i.e., the landscape, the city, and the architecture (Wu Liangyong, 1994b, 1996a).

In 1997, Wu Liangyong pointed out when summarizing the research results that: "when the continuity of geographical environment and changes of human and material environments affect the nature and our settlement, special regional human settlement will be formed; therefore, we should study regional transport network, regional urban network, integrated urban and rural township pattern, and open spatial system from two aspects of both historical and current status."

Since 1994, the NSFC has sponsored and organized a series of seminars on human settlements (Kunming 1994, Xi'an 1995, Guangzhou 1996, Chongqing 1998), promoting academic discussions in the field. From 1999 onward, the NSFC has sponsored Wu Liangyong to launch a research project titled "Basic Theories and Typical Cases of Sustainable Development of Human Settlements in China" (the key project during the 9th Five-Year-Plan), which was then integrated with the key research project organized by the State Ministry of Construction, "Studies on Urban and Rural Spatial Development Planning in Beijing-Tianjin-North Hebei (the Greater Beijing Area)", trying to apply the scientific theories on human settlements on regional spatial planning, exploring in an innovative way the methods of realizing integrated and harmonious regional development, having great significance as a model project on the development of regional planning during a new era.

A.2.2.5   Drafting UIA Beijing Charter Based on Theories on the Science of Human Settlements (1999)

The XX UIA World Congress 1999 adopted the Beijing Charter composed under the leadership of Wu Liangyong. The Beijing Charter guides architects to have a comprehensive understanding on the methodology of human settlement instead of being restricted in the narrow scope of applied aesthetics so as to integrate studies on architecture, landscape, and city planning, to include the architectural processes of new construction, operation, maintenance, and even innovation, while remaining rooted in local culture and society, covering multiple levels of technical systems in the psychological field, combining fine arts, handicraft, industrial design, and the work of architects, sticking to professional ethics of taking the entire society as the top owner, and managing to realize open and continuous education on architecture available to all people. The Beijing Charter is an important document of the XX UIA World Congress and an important guideline for future development of the world architecture community. The scientific core of the document is actually the academic research result of Wu Liangyong and the summary of his studies on the general architecture and the science of human settlements (Mao Qizhi, 2000).

A.2.2.6   Publishing Introduction to Human Settlement Science (2001)

In 2001, Wu Liangyong published "Introduction to Human Settlement Science", exploring possible development goals, analyzing and deciding on solutions and action guidelines applicable to regions with different conditions, and proposing several study frameworks, which further consolidate the foundation for the studies of human settlement science. According to "Introduction to Human Settlement Science": (1) the core of human settlements is people and the studies shall focus on people; (2) nature is the foundation of human settlement; for production, living of people, and specific activities of constructing human settlements must be done in the broad background of nature, and ecological environment shall include the settlements for all creatures including human beings; (3) the science of human settlement studies the relationship among human settlements as well as the composition of multiple disciplines. The book indicates that the general theories on architecture proposed by Wu Liangyong have been developed into a broader outlook of human settlements.

In October 2000, the Chinese Society for Urban Studies organized in Beijing the Seminar on Human Settlement Construction, serving as a platform of communications in the field of urban human settlements construction in China. In April and May 2002, the Chinese Society for Urban Studies joined hands with Shanghai Research Center of Urban Development Information, Tsinghua University, and Architectural Society of China and organized in Beijing two sessions of the Seminar on the Science of Human Settlements and Urban Development, studying the theories on human settlements proposed by Wu Liangyong, and discussing such issues of how to meet the requirements of national economic and social growth in city planning, designing, and construction, how to realize sustainable development, as well as the principles of constructing favorable urban ecological environment.

In March 2001, the guidelines of the national 10th Five-Year-Plan, in view of creating reasonable urban systems were as follows: the focus is to create favorable human settlements, to reinforce the construction of urban ecology and the comprehensive treatment of pollution, and to improve urban environment. This is the first time that China raised in its official document the concept of "human settlements". With years of efforts and exploration made by both domestic and international academic communities, the construction of human settlements has become one of the important contents of national construction, which indicates that the theories on human settlements proposed by Wu Liangyong have formally taken shape.

A.2.3   The Stage of Blossoming (After 2003)

Since 2003, China started comprehensive reforms aiming to improve the socialist market-oriented economic system. The Chinese society has entered the stage of structural transition, and urbanization has progressed rapidly. These realities require a scientific outlook on development to coordinate and direct urban and rural growth. Accordingly, the theories on human settlements initiated by Wu Liangyong have also progressed together with the times.

A.2.3.1   The Application of Human Settlement Theories on Regional Spatial Planning

As early as 1992, Wu Liangyong proposed to "extend the research scope from cities to regions"(Wu Liangyong, 1992). After the theories on human settlements took shape, they have been applied in the research of regional planning in Beijing-Tianjin-Hebei Area and the Yangtze River Delta Area. Human settlement becomes an important content of regional planning: on the one hand, it enriches the theories of regional planning; on the other hand, the theories on human settlements have also progressed accordingly.

(1) Human Settlement and Regional Planning

At the annual meeting on city planning held in 2004, Wu Liangyong delivered an academic report, "The Concept of Region and Some Thoughts on Human Settlement" (Wu Liangyong, 2005b). At the Seminar on Regional Planning (Ningbo) organized by National Development and Reform Commission on March 25, 2005, Wu Liangyong further pointed out that, in view of the science of human settlements, regional planning expects to: ① apply the scientific outlook on development in spatial development; ② stick to spatial integration and mutual coordination; ③ stick to the concept of a people-centered harmonious society; ④ protect, treat, and develop natural ecology; ⑤ protect, develop, and revive cultural ecology; and ⑥ further promote the application of human settlement theories in solving urban and rural problems (Wu Liangyong, 2005c). In fact, regional planners want to apply theories on human settlements in their planning work. In 2006, Wu Liangyong was in charge of a study project centering on the application of human settlements science and published the research results, "Studies on Urban and Rural Spatial Development Planning in Beijing-Tianjin-Hebei Area" (Second-Phase Report) (Wu Liangyong, *et al*, 2006b).

(2) Regional Studies applying Theories on Human Settlements

Meanwhile, Wu Liangyong supervised his PhD candidates on launching a series of studies on human settlements focusing on regional spatial issues, including: "Regional Features of Architecture and Cities: A Study on Regional Architecture Based on Human Settlement Concepts" (Shan Jun, 2002), "On the Forms and Construction of Human Settlement in Haidai Area before Qin Dynasty" (Zhang Yue, 2003), "Suburban Development Based on Regional Integration: What shall Rapidly Urbanized Beijing Learn from Paris" (Liu Jian, 2003), "Shangrila, Utopia, and Ideal City: A Study on Human Settlement in Shangrila Area" (Zhai Hui, 2005), "On Spatial Development of the Corridor Area in Beijing and Tianjin: Its History, Present, and Future" (Zhao Liang, 2006), "Theories and Practice of Strategic Spatial Planning in China: A Case Study of Tianjin and Beijing-Tianjin-Hebei Area" (Huo Bing, 2006), "Ecological Security and Human Settlement: A Case Study on Northwest Yunnan Province" (Ou Xiaokun, 2006), "The Treatment of Loess Plateau Area in North Shaanxi Province and the Applicable Pattern for Spatial Form Evolution of Human Settlement" (Zhou Qinghua, 2006), and "On Urban Spatial Development in China Based on Territory" (Wang Kai, 2006), making the application of the science of human settlements in regional space a new and promising research direction.

A.2.3.2   The Application of Human Settlement Theories in Construction Projects

In recent years, one of the features of development in human settlement studies in China is their application in some mega projects, such as the Three Gorges Project and South-to-North Diversion Project, while the construction of these projects also expands the application scope of the science of human settlements.

(1) Three Gorges Project and human settlement studies

The Three Gorges Project is the largest ever construction project since the People's Republic of China was founded in 1949 and the the largest water conservancy hub project in the world as well. The project has the following features: complicated technologies, large amount of investment, large amount of relocated residents, difficult task of moving and relocation, long period of time for restoring environment during the late stage of project, and the large area involved. The project plans to make a large-scale adjustment to and construction of the production, living, and ecological environments in an area (water and land) of more than 50,000 km^2 with nearly 14 million people in the early 21st Century. In fact, this is a comprehensive and systematic project aiming to realize the sustainable development of newly constructed human settlements in the entire area. From 1994 to 1996, Wu Liangyong and other scholars proposed to study the issues concerning the Three Gorges Project from the perspective of human settlement science, so as to take into full consideration the complicated situations of project construction. They studied on an integrated basis the technological, social, and cultural elements as well as the construction of the project and the sustainable development of human settlements in the area. They focused on creating city space suitable for the regional environment according to the features of cities and architecture in Three Gorges Area. They proposed to the central government that the construction of human settlements in the area shall be emphasized on a timely basis with practical directions as well as corresponding implementation measures and regulations before allocating responsibilities and duties to local administrations and technical authorities

(Wu Liangyong, Zhao Wanmin, 1995, 1997; Zhao Wanmin, 1996).

(2) Studies on construction environment of South-to-North Diversion Central Trunk Line Project

From 2005 to 2007, Wu Liangyong was in charge of the "Engineering Environment Planning on South-to-North Water Diversion Central Trunk Line Project". The central trunk line project is an important part of the South-to-North Diversion Project, a water resource development and utilization project centering on water supply with multiple tasks of flood control, electricity generation, and ecological environment improvement in several river basins, and a key fundamental strategic facility solving the problem of tight water supply in Beijing, Tianjin, and the entire North China. The trunk canal of the project starts from Taochaqu of the Danjiangkou Reservoir, crosses 655 rivers in four basins of the Yangtze River, Huaihe River, Yellow River, and Haihe River, and finally reaches Tuancheng Lake in Beijing, with a total length of 1,277 km. In view of spatial planning of the central trunk line project, the planners face a series of specific issues of land acquisition, ecological construction, cultural protection, settlement construction, and urbanization, and the solutions must be based on an integrated and unified spatial planning. In view of the studies concerning "Engineering Environment Planning on South-to-North Water Diversion Central Trunk Line Project", Wu Liangyong applied the science of human settlements to study on a comprehensive basis issues such as the protection and construction of ecological environment affected by the project, the protection and construction of historical cultural environment, and the characteristics of the buildings of large water conservancy projects, focusing especially on the project spatial planning, the establishing of ecological security patter, the creation of architectural images, and proposing general planning and designing regulations on architecture environment so as to control and guide the overall image and specific details of the entire project (Wu Liangyong, *et al*, 2007).

A.2.3.3   Scientific Outlook on Development and Science of Human Settlements

(1) Five Overall Considerations and the Studies of Human Settlement Science

The Report to the Sixteenth National Congress of the Communist Party of China proposes the great goal of "building a well-off society in an all-round way", and the Third Plenary Session of the Sixteenth CPC Central Committee proposed to "take overall considerations on urban and rural development, development among regions, economic and social development, relations between man and nature, and domestic development and opening to the outside world." Wu Liangyong takes all these as the general guidelines for economic and social growth in China as well as the top principle guiding the construction of human settlements in this country, which shall therefore be attached significant importance. Wu Liangyong also reflects on previous studies in the field and further promotes the understanding on the development of human settlement science: ① five principles, five main elements, and five levels proposed in his "Introduction to Human Settlement Science" are based on the above-mentioned "five overall considerations"; ② to study again the unified planning and designing of human settlements, integrating different regions, urban and rural areas, cities, communities, and architecture, taking into consideration these inter-related parts as a whole, applying comprehensive multi-disciplinary perspectives to set up principles on a systematic planning at different levels; and ③ to study the path of urbanization in China from the perspective of achieving a harmonious urban and rural development, advocating a gradual transition toward an integrated and harmonious growth in both cities and countryside (Wu Liangyong, 2004d, 2005a).

(2) The Transition of Development Pattern and the Exploration of Human Settlement Science

The report to the Seventeenth National Congress of the Communist Party of China proposes to "change development pattern", and Wu Liangyong further elaborates that in view of the problems concerning the construction of human settlements, modern society has learned lessons from the past and requires to change development patterns so as to realize sustainable development. The construction of human settlements in China must be based on actual conditions and situations in the country. With the principle of adopting a scientific outlook on development, we should carry out two basic tasks: one is to center on people and to base on social and public life; the other is to construct human settlements by sticking to the principle of achieving "conservation culture". Accordingly, we would gain a better understanding on human settlements at different levels, taking into overall consideration the regional coordination and harmonious urban and rural development. We should take a problem-oriented perspective to launch multi-disciplinary studies on architecture, cities, landscape, and technologies, and should further develop and integrate cross-disciplinary studies. We should absorb the essence of Chinese culture so as to realize the comprehensive innovation of human settlement culture, creating urban cultures with distinct regional features. We should stick to the methodology of generative holism; gather all social wisdom, making it a common understanding in the entire society instead of in the science community before further promoting it into a common understanding among policy makers, gradually and steadily improving the science of human settlements (Wu Liangyong, 2008).

A.2.3.4 Studies on Human Settlement Culture

Culture is the combination of both material and spiritual wealth. The improvement of human settlement construction quality refers to the improvement of material wealth on the one hand and the recreation of living culture and cultural environment on the other hand. Cultural studies concerning human settlements, especially the exploration of Chinese architectural and urban culture, have always been the focus of work for Wu Liangyong. Since 2003, cultural studies on human settlements made by Wu Liangyong have had three distinct features.

(1) Combining human settlement culture with globalization, urbanization, and modernization

Different regions have different cultures; Chinese cities grow in different regions and have been nurtured by different regional cultures. China is at a great turning point in history, facing the invasion and impact of incoming "dominant" cultures, resulting in the lack of inner vitality of "weak" regional cultures, which have no specific development directions and self-awareness of improvement. Without conscious protection and development, these regional cultures will easily become passive, lose creativity and competitiveness, and will finally be devoured by the great wave of "cultural assimilation" in the world. Therefore, the studies on human settlement culture shall grasp the general trend of globalization, and pay attention to the heritage and innovation of regional and traditional cultures (Wu Liangyong, 2004c). From 2004 to 2005, Wu Liangyong was in charge of studies of urban cultures, a sub-theme of the research project on "Sustainable Development Strategy during the Progress of Urbanization in China's ponsored by the Chinese Academy of Engineering, summarizing urgent issues facing modern urban cultures as follows: ① emphasizing economic growth, ignoring the spirit of humanity; ② emphasizing elite cultures, ignoring public caring; ③ emphasizing construction scale, ignoring overall coordination; ④ emphasizing comparison and renovation, ignoring cultural features; ⑤ emphasizing presentable looks, ignoring institutional improvement; and ⑥ emphasizing partial effect, ignoring long-term goals. It is recommended that studies shall pay attention to the fields of humanity during the progress of urbanization, that the construction projects shall have an overall perspective, and that the planners shall emphasize the construction of urban cultures at different levels. In 2003, Wu Liangyong studied the theories of Zhang Jian and the modern development of Nantong city, compared it with the modern history of western cities, concluded that Nantong is the first city in Modern China and that Zhang Jian had made great contributions to the creation of city patterns during early stage of modernization progress in China on the basis of regional cultures (Wu Liangyong, et al, 2006). He supervised his PhD candidates in the specialized study in the field, producing the thesis of "A Tentative Study on the History of Modern City Planning and Construction in Nantong and on Zhang Jian's Theories on City Planning" (Yu Haiyi, 2005).

(2) Emphasizing the relationship among the protection of urban culture, the planning, and the construction

The progress of globalization, urbanization, and modernization has resulted in the rapid changes of traditional values, making urban cultural heritages face unprecedented conflicts of protection and development. Since 2003, Wu Liangyong has put forward several times such issues of cultural transformation, historical cultural protection, and innovative culture creation. Wu Liangyong delivered a speech titled "The Protection of Cultural Heritages and the Creation of Cultural Environment" on June 9, 2007, proposing "Active Protection and Overall Development"(Wu Liangyong, 2007).

Meanwhile, he supervised some of his PhD candidates to focus their studies in the field, producing "Cultural Planning: An Approach Promoting Comprehensive City Development by Using Cultural Resources" (Huang He, 2005), "A Theoretical Study on City Reviving in Western Europe and Its Enlightenment on China' (Wu Chen, 2005), and "The Protection of Cultural Heritage and the Construction of City Culture" (Shan Jixiang, 2008). Currently, the studies focus on cultural protection and planned construction in Beijing and Nanjing, among other cities.

(3) Improving the excavation of cultural heritages to a higher level of independent innovation

Chinese civilization enjoys a long history, leaving a large amount of cultural heritages with significant historical and scientific values. In order to further explore, collect, and study the values of these heritages, to fully demonstrate ancient inventions and creations in China, to promote the protection of cultural heritages and independent innovation, the State Administration of Cultural Heritage launched in 2005 the "Project Compass: Exploration and Presentation of the Values of Chinese Ancient Inventions and Creations". On April 21, 2006, Wu Liangyong pointed out at the consulting meeting of the project that: human settlement reflects the consolidation of time, space, and people, as well as the development and changes of the times, the society, and the ideology, and the combination of technologies and human sciences. He recommended adding the content of studying the development and evolution of human settlements in China as well as the system of construction, so as to enrich and improve the results and content of "Exploration and Presentation of the Values of Chinese Ancient Inventions and Creations Project". In 2007, Wu Liangyong was in charge of two research projects, "Exploration and Presentation of Ancient Human Settlements Invention and Creation" and "Studies on Scientific Values of Invention and Creation Cultural Heritages in Ancient Human Settlements: Trial Case Studies of Chengdu Plain Areas". Accordingly, systematic studies on the history of human settlements development in China have also been launched, managing to provide new sources for the construction of modern human settlements.

A.2.3.5   Exploration of "Disciplinary Cluster"

Human settlement is a frontier branch of academic studies in the world, and the science of human settlements initiated by Wu Liangyong is actually a disciplinary cluster. The 201st Xiangshan Science Conference was held in Beijing from April 2 to 4, 2003 with the theme "Scientific Issues of Urban Development in China". As one of the executive chairmen, Wu Liangyong appealed for the study of the key scientific issues concerning urban development. Since 2006, being sponsored by Beijing Municipal Commission of Education, Wu Liangyong was in charge of the research project "City Planning Construction and Management" (2006-2008), a project of constructing disciplinary cluster in higher education institutions in Beijing launched under the guidance of the scientific outlook on development and on sustainable development so as to create a bright future of urban development in Beijing and to solve key issues that arose during the process of development and construction of the city. The research project is extremely difficult and shall be conducted on a comprehensive basis and during a long period of time. At the work meeting held on September 18, 2006, Wu Liangyong pointed out that: "The construction and management of Beijing city planning is a complicated issue, making it extremely difficult to be solved by depending on the government alone. Currently, we conduct cross-disciplinary studies by constructing disciplinary cluster so as to create an academic research environment, to facilitate the reaching of common understanding on some key issues, and to finally promote the municipal government in making decisions. Accordingly, one of the important tasks of setting up disciplinary cluster is to construct an academic community." The setting up of a disciplinary cluster depends mainly on Tsinghua University, which is supported by Beijing University of Technology, Beijing University of Civil Engineering and Architecture, and National Capital Planning Commission. At present, the organization structure and working mechanism have been established, and the work has been conducted on an orderly basis according to plans.

In August 2007, the Chinese Society for Urban Studies proposed "to construct and improve the disciplinary system on urban studies under the guidance of the science of human settlements, holding that 'Introduction to Human Settlement Science' written by Academician Wu Liangyong makes a complete and comprehensive elaboration and analysis on the theories of human settlement science, which lays a solid foundation in view of theories and methodology for setting up and improve disciplinary system on urban studies. We should continuously improve the theories during the practice so as to set up the disciplinary system on urban studies with distinct Chinese characteristics" (Zhou Ganzhi, 2007). In 2007, Wu Liangyong supervised his PhD candidates in finishing the PhD Dissertation "Dilemma of and Solution to Positive Science in City Planning" (He Xinghua, 2007).

A.3 Features of Theories on Human Settlements

The theories on the science of human settlements proposed by Wu Liangyong actively face the realities and advocate environmental designing, showing clearly the love of the society and the people as well as the respect for excellent cultural heritages that people have created.

A.3.1 Applying Theories to Serve the Society and the Public

In view of the formation process of theories on human settlements, Wu Liangyong has had to deal with a lot of problems that occurred during urban and rural construction. On the one hand, he was anxious and even angry facing these realities and could not help talking about them (Wu Liangyong, 2003c); but on the other hand, he had dreams of future development of the country, planning in advance and making corresponding preparations. He actively took part in actual construction projects by making use of various conditions, devoting time to theoretical explorations, solving in a creative way a series of issues that arose during the construction of human settlements in China, and also developing on a continuous basis his theories on human settlements.

A.3.1.1 An Applied Study

Most of the scientific studies on human settlements made by Wu Liangyong have focused on actual problems in China. For example, his studies on Ju'er Hutong in Beijing aimed to solve the conflicts between the protection of the old town and modern construction, to explore the theoretical methods to coordinate the protection and the construction; "there are hundreds of important and famous historical cities in China, so one of the most urgent tasks is to create a social housing to not only meet the requirements of comfortable modern life but also closely relate to original historical environment"(Wu Liangyong, 1994e). His study report on "Today and Tomorrow of China Construction Industry" focuses on the issues concerning construction that arose during the process of rapid social and economic growth in the 1980s in China.

Meanwhile, Wu Liangyong believes that the science of human settlements is an applied study serving the society and people. In view of the formation process of theories on human settlements initiated by Wu Liangyong, the science of human settlements is a farsighted scientific methodology of general architecture created on the basis of social requirements by continuously summarizing practical experience, abstracting into theories before applying in realities so as to test these theories. In his "Introduction to Human Settlement Science", Wu Liangyong summarizes basic theories from realities and seeks specific solutions to actual issues that arose during the process of human settlements development in China and in the world with his keen insight and vision. In view of the problems concerning the construction of human settlements, Wu Liangyong has made a lot of proposals with great values, which were emphasized and accepted by authorities and leaders, enjoying great social influence. For example, Wu Liangyong proposed "to develop medium-sized cities'in 1979, which was adopted and contributed to the state policy of "reasonably developing medium-sized cities". He contributed in 1983 to the making of technical policy on "the construction of housing, environment, and cities" and proposed in 1985 the principles on the construction and planning related to the Beijing Asian Games, both of which were accorded great importance by relevant authorities. In May 1998, Wu Liangyong and other scholars proposed several "Suggestions on Emphasizing Integral and Systematic Regional Development in Developed Areas" on the basis of studies on areas in south Jiangsu Province, studying the progress of urbanization in Eastern China, summarizing relevant experience and seven suggestions on how to solve existing problems, including the construction of the science of human settlements so as to meet the upcoming wave of urbanization during the new century. In February 2000, Wu Liangyong and other scholars proposed two suggestions on urban construction in the "Report on City Planning and Construction of Sanya", which have been approved by Zhu Rongji, Li Lanqing, Wen Jiabao from the State Council, as well as Yu Zhengsheng and Zhao Baojiang from the State Ministry of Construction. In June 2001, Wu Liangyong and Zhou Ganzhi wrote a letter to Prime Minister Zhu Rongji, pointing out the problems concerning city planning and making suggestions on improving urban and rural planning work. Zhu Rongji instructed the proposal to be submitted to the work meeting organized by the prime minister and the authority involved to prepare a document. Wen Jiabao instructed the State Ministry of Construction to prepare the document and that city planning and construction must follow strict regulations so as to solve the current status of chaos and existing problems completely. It was also suggested that the situations and problems should be reported to the State Council and that the law on city planning should be revised as soon as possible. In January 2002, the leaders of the State Council listened to the reports made by the State Ministry of Construction, and in May 2002, the State Council issued a "Circular on Strengthening the Supervision and Management of Urban and Rural Planning" (Guo Fa [2002] No.13), clarifying the requirements on prominent problems in urban and rural planning and construction and on future planning work (Wang Guangtao, 2004).

A.3.1.2   A Future Based on Dreams

Facing complicated problems and numerous difficulties, Wu Liangyong has always had dreams for future. He believes that, "dreams nurture aspiration and human society progresses continuously by chasing numerous dreams; a dream will finally come true with efforts." He believes in a future based on dreams: "We're looking forward to a great country, to a stable and happy life, to the coming of the new century, to a better human settlement, which will not happen without our efforts; we should explore future development by working hard and consciously, which requires absorbing all beautiful dreams"(Wu Liangyong, 1996c). It is obvious that to construct better human settlements is another dream cherished by Wu Liangyong and the hope urging him to make long-term exploration in the field. The belief on a future based on dreams serves as a source of optimistic theories on human settlements for Wu Liangyong.

A.3.1.3   Being a Doer with Aspiration

In November 1993, Wu Liangyong urged at the Annual Conference on City Planning in China (Xiangfan) that, "we should be doers with aspiration," "in the history of city planning, there were a lot of idealist thinkers; they were sensitive to new things, had visions for the future. But they were not merely talkers; instead, they were active doers devoting to reforms and practice … The planners must have sublime ideals, virtues, and personality, must be those combining idealism with realism. Without ideals, a plan will have no soul; but without consideration of realities, a plan will be empty doctrine without any practical significance"(Wu Liangyong, 1994c).

This is in fact the principle that Wu Liangyong has always abided by. As early as 1989 and in "Conclusion of A General Theory of Architecture", he pointed out clearly that: "Architects must be in possession of the qualities of both an idealist and a realist," "in history and today, there are a lot of outstanding architects, whose theories, philosophies shine together with their excellent works." He further pointed out that "the leading feature of their specialty is not that they were sitting there talking and waiting for the goals to be realized automatically, instead they devoted wholeheartedly to the realities and explored actively all possibilities to make their dreams come true."

With regard to construction of human settlements, Wu Liangyong introduced his theories by integrating specific city planning work. On March 26, 1994, Wu Liangyong proposed to the mayor of Suzhou to construct "a new paradise". He pointed out that there should be an idealistic action agenda for the construction of the "new paradise" in the 21st Century, which is the idealist aspect of the project, while at the same time, every specific measure shall be based on realities, which is the realistic aspect of the project. Without ideals, the project will be shortsighted; but without the solid foundation of realism, the project will become an empty talk.[1] Since 2000, Wu Liangyong has studied

---

[1] Wu Liangyong, "Reviving the Historical Glories of Oriental Water City: On Regional Development, Ancient Town Protection, and Architectural Cultural Creation of Suzhou Urban Area", Embracing the New Century: Collection of Works by Wu Liangyong on Urban Studies, China Architecture and Building Press, 1996.

Zhang Jian and his theories on the first modern city of Nantong. He pointed out that: "Zhang Jian emphasized both ideal and practice; from his articles, we can see his ideals in urban and rural construction. At the same time, he was also a doer and devoted his entire life to realizing most of what he planned and designed in a changing political and economic society. His theories on city planning have been gradually formed with clear track that we can follow today... It's rare that, with limited conditions at the time, Zhang Jian had followed the path of active progressing and independent innovation and became a doer with great achievements ... The spirit and courage of pioneer is inspiring."❶All these comments show that Wu Liangyong encourages scholars to be doers with ideals, to apply theories in practice, and to manage to improve human settlements.

A.3.1.4　Developing Theories during the Process of Solving Difficult Issues Creatively

The experience of human settlement construction has been a dynamic source promoting the formation and development of the science of human settlements and the theories on human settlements can be summarized as follows: to start from the actual conditions in China, to study the objective rules of urban and rural development in this country, to stick to the application of theories in actual work, and to serve the construction of human settlements in China. For example, Wu Liangyong studied the construction of human settlements in the Three Gorges Area with resource environment being threatened, the construction of landscape city of Sanya under the condition of rapid economic and social growth, and the construction of human settlements in Northwestern Yunnan Province with limited ecological conditions.

Wu Liangyong could always find problems in actual practice and further improve the academic studies on human settlements. Accordingly, the science of human settlements has progressed continuously during the process of solving difficult issues of the time. For example, the renovation of endangered houses and a new courtyard house complex at the Ju'er Hutong in Beijing accomplished in 1992 explored the way of renovating the old town, "created a new way of renovating the old town of Beijing while keeping and improving the traditional courtyard house

---

❶ Wu Liangyong, "Reviving the Historical Glories of Oriental Water City: On Regional Development, Ancient Town Protection, and Architectural"

complex pattern, managing to protect a large amount of old buildings in the old town from being demolished and removed, and exploring a new way for local residents in historical cities to participate in both the planning and the construction.[1] In 1999, the UIA adopted the Beijing Charter, which, on the basis of the background of great development and great changes in the 20th Century and facing such problems of urbanization serving as a double-bladed sword and the loss of architectural soul, proposed the road map to effectively solve the difficult issue of holism for the world architecture community from the perspectives of "general architecture" and "science of human settlements". As a result, the science of human settlements in China has been accepted by the world academic community. It is expected that the further development of theories on human settlements will also be based on meeting the actual social needs and on solving actual problems during the process of constructing human settlements.

A.3.2 Designing Environment

People need a beautiful environment to live in, and human settlements are the results of designing and architectural construction made by human beings on land. One of the most significant aspects of the theories on human settlements of Wu Liangyong is to apply technical methods of planning and designing to improve the quality of human settlements. Wu Liangyong believes that: "As for architectural creation activities conducted by people, they include not only the building of houses, but also the construction of living and working environments, the creation of beautiful urban and rural environments, which makes them the construction of both material and spiritual civilizations". "Urban and rural settlements are the biggest works of art."

A.3.2.1 Artistic Conception of the Environment

Human settlement is a gigantic material space in physical form and with invisible form as well; it has artistic beauty beyond its physical form. Since his young age, Wu Liangyong was greatly attracted to fine arts. At college, he received academic education on architecture at the Fine Arts Institute of Paris and had deep understanding on the artistic conception of Zong Baihua, Fu Baoshi, Xu Beihong, Qi Baishi, and other Chinese masters. During his study at Cranbrook Academy of Arts in the US, he learned

---

[1] Remarks on the World Habitat Award, 1992.

architecture and city planning from Saarinen as well as some other courses of painting and sculpture, which helped him to greatly improve both his artistic taste and vision. He has always considered the amazing architectural space and beautiful urban and rural environments as the greatest creations by mankind and has managed to express them in artistic forms. Accordingly, he takes the construction of human settlements as both his academic pursuit and part of his life dedicating to art. In other words, Wu Liangyong has benefited a lot from two majors: he learns from paintings the architecture, the cities, and the human settlement, and then he observes nature and experiences life from an artistic perspective, seeking the point of intersection between the two majors. He seeks ways to combine architectursque, meaning of paintings, artistic conception, and artistic vision and to create "the artistic conception of the environment".

Wu Liangyong has mentioned several times the concept of "architectursque" proposed by Liang Sicheng and Lin Huiyin in their article "On Architecture in Suburban Areas of Beijing" published in 1932. The couple was keen on finding the architectursque in Chinese architecture, which was several decades earlier than the concept of genius loci proposed by Norberg-Schulz in the west. Wu Liangyong pointed out that, in the history of human settlements construction in China, many cities including Fuzhou, Changshu, Zhenjiang, and Hangzhou have different artistic beauties thanks to the combination with their respective natural conditions, which can be found in literary chorography of these cities as well as a few city maps (Wu Liangyong, 2000a). He also emphasizes "the touch of shrine" shown in special commemorative places, arguing that the environment and content of a building will change along with visitors, time, and place, leaving different impressions on different visitors. The "touch of shrine" refers to the impressive spiritual strength that an architectural environment has, making people feel the sacredness, and this is the artistic conception of a place (known as genius loci, but the term of "artistic conception" is more appropriate).[1]

A.3.2.2   Aesthetic Exploration on Human Settlements

Wu Liangyong studies human settlements from an artistic perspective,

---

[1] Wu Liangyong, A Touch of Shrine and a Touch of Sculpture, the speech delivered at the Seminar on Yellow Emperor Mausoleum, 7 April 2006.

believing that the art of settlements features the beauty of integrity, changes, distinct characteristics, and rich content [1]. He also emphasizes "Exploring Distinct Beauty of a City" (Wu Liangyong, 2002a). For example, his studies on the city of Beijing, whether the issues of the protection and creation of historical cultural settlements or the construction of new settlements, have taken aesthetic perspective, which is shown in his articles "Promoting the Great Order of the Capital City, Reviving Beijing as an Ancient Capital" (Wu Liangyong, 1994d), "On the Changing Ancient Capital", and "On Zhongguancun: With More Aesthetic Thinking", which are some of his master works.

With regard to the actual construction of human settlements, Wu Liangyong paid special attention to the promotion and application of Chinese heritages and advocated gaining inspiration from traditional philosophy on human settlements for designing modern cities (Wu Liangyong, 2000b). From a Fuzhou map drawn during the Qing Dynasty that he collected, Wu Liangyong explored the aesthetic principles and relevant issues concerning oriental cities (Wu Liangyong, 2000a). In view of specific architectural designing, he derived inspiration from profound ancient cultural tradition and then transformed these into concrete forms (for details please refer to the section "Culture Infiltration").

A.3.2.3 Development of Landscape

The general background of the theories on human settlements initiated by Wu Liangyong is that the rapid economic and social growth and urbanization have greatly affected urban and rural ecological and cultural environment. L. Mumford concluded on "four explosions", that is, the explosions of population, of suburban areas, of high-speed trunk roads, and of recreational areas. The construction of human settlements, including buildings, cities, regions, gardens, and landscape, has undergone tremendous changes in spatial size, a quantitative change has led finally to qualitative changes, which requires us to make the focus, content, and methods of construction projects to be in accordance with the changes, among which recognizing and returning to nature is the most important.

Wu Liangyong believes that the natural landscape of mountains and waters in

---

[1] Wu Liangyong, General Theories of Architecture: An Artistic Perspective, Tsinghua University Press, 1989.

China contains rich cultural connotations. The culture centering on famous mountains is based on aesthetics of different philosophies and combines with the artistic conception of traditional Chinese poems and paintings, producing distinct characteristics. One will have a better understanding of the beauty of both the sky and the earth after studying the gardens and landscape in both the west and in China (Wu Liangyong, 2003a). In 2003, Wu Liangyong pointed out at the opening ceremony of the Department of Landscape Architecture, School of Architecture, Tsinghua University, that: "We should use the resources that the Center for Human Settlements has accumulated for years and the advantage of cross-disciplinary studies to promote the development of the science of human settlements, to actively protect famous scenery sites and natural resources from being destroyed by rapid growth of tourism, and more importantly, to emphasize the protection and development of natural resources, to expand the initial results of promoting national scenery sites."

A.3.2.4 The Artistic Layout of Urban Space

For city planning, Wu Liangyong advocates combining actual local conditions of both mountains and waters so as to achieve artistic layout of urban space. For example, in 1995, Wu Liangyong proposed the overall planning pattern of "Landscape in Four Corners" in the shape of a cross for the city of Suzhou. In 2002, for the overall planning of historical areas in Jinan by using the traditional city planning method of arranging architecture along the central axes, Wu Liangyong proposed "to take the mountains located in distance as the gap, to dig the North Lake, and to create a new district". He also proposed to plan and construct Quehua Historical and Cultural Park in Jinan. In 2003, in view of the studies on the Beijing city spatial development strategy, Wu Liangyong took into full consideration the features, history, and culture of mountains and waters in Beijing, proposing an overall layout with two axes and two belts, four parks, and multiple centers, and the construction of four suburban wild parks around the city in Xishan Mountain, Jundu Mountain, Chaobai River-Wenyu River, and Nanyuan. During the studies on the Tianjin city spatial development strategy and the compilation of overall city planning, Wu Liangyong proposed to protect the wetland resources in both the south and the north of the city so as to create an overall layout "with spring water in south and north areas and flocks of gulls coming everyday". All these proposals were made under the principle of integrated and sustainable urban and rural development and have been adopted and applied in city spatial development planning. In this way, Wu Liangyong explores the new pattern of constructing human settlements realizing several objectives of protecting nature, repairing the ecology, promoting the culture, and reviving the landscape. During this period of time, he also supervised his PhD candidates in studying the "Theory on Recreation with Human Settlement Perspective and A Study on Development Strategy" (Wang Yu, 2006).

A.3.3   Caring for the Public

The core of human settlement is people, and so the studies on human settlement shall satisfy the needs of living, which is one of the most fundamental preconditions for the studies of the science of human settlements (Wu Liangyong, 2001a). When he was a teenager, Wu Liangyong experienced internal conflicts and foreign invasion during wartime. Then he was nurtured by the homeland and the people, a personal experience that has given him great regard for people, which was seen in his theories on human settlements later.

A.3.3.1   Constructing Beautiful Human Settlements and Society at the Same Time

To create a good human settlement has been a century old dream cherished by human beings and a basic need for them as well. In the 20th Century, it took people more than half a century to recognize the importance of human settlements and one of the significant contents is to improve settlements for the public and the society. Wu Liangyong argues that the reason why people construction human habitat is to take care of people in the first place; the goal of constructing human settlements is "to build habitat that can be developed on a sustainable basis, to create good and healthy settlements with cultural connotation for people".

The construction of human settlements is closely related to social lives and the theories of Wu Liangyong on human settlements contain profound social responsibilities. In the "Conclusion to A General Theory of Architecture" published in 1989, he pointed out: "A beautiful architectural environment is created together with beautiful social ideals and is the field where social ideals join with social construction." In 1999, at the XX UIA World Congress, Wu Liangyong proposed once again "to create beautiful architectural environment and ideal society at the same time", holding that "a beautiful world will cease existing without a good architectural environment, for the good order of environment reflects a good social order."

A.3.3.2   Caring for Livelihood

The construction of human settlements aims to provide settlements for the public, including residential communities in a broad sense and housing in a narrow sense. Wu Liangyong has mentioned several times that in 1951, facing the problem of focusing on the construction of landmark buildings while ignoring ordinary buildings, the Beijing City Planning Committee invited him to make a speech on the housing in Beijing at a team meeting. On the request of Lin Huiyin, Wu Liangyong made investigations on residential communities in the Huashi area, studying the housing issues of poverty stricken people there. In the early 1960s, being affected by the order that "no city planning is allowed in three years", the City Planning Teaching and Research Group of Department of Architecture, Tsinghua University, started to study housing issues and turned to care for livelihood, accumulating experience in the planning of residential communities and the designing of residential buildings, exploring ways to reduce construction cost and construction term by starting from underground construction work. Since then, to study social housing projects, especially to emphasize the studies on endangered houses, flooded houses and courtyards, and the houses suffering rain leakage, has become a tradition and characteristic of academic studies on architecture at Tsinghua University. On May 26, 1995, Wu Liangyong made it clear that: to establish the Center for Human Settlements is to study two important issues of urbanization and housing.[1] In fact, these are also two global tasks, as the United Nations Conference on Human Settlements (known as Habitat II) held in June 1996 addressed two themes of equal global importance: "Adequate shelter for all" and "Sustainable human settlements

---

[1] Note made by Zuo Chuan, May 26, 1995.

development in an urbanizing world".

China is the most populous country in the world and has to take great efforts to meet the demand for housing and to improve the quality of housing. Taking into consideration the actual conditions and in order to fulfill his long-cherished dream of providing housing for people to live a happy live, Wu Liangyong proposed the issues of housing security and rural living security. During the meeting with Minister Yu Zhengsheng of Construction held on November 27, 1997, Wu Liangyong pointed out that: "A country must have a unified housing policy with various standards from high to low; there should be social housing projects instead of depending solely on commercial developers to take control of land resources… One of the basic principles is that China shall not promote the housing type of villa. Currently, rural housing issues haven't been solved. But there should be both urban and rural housing systems so as to carry out the sustainable development."[1] At the meeting with Party Committee Secretary Jiang Weixin of the State Ministry of Construction held on September 6, 2007, Wu Liangyong advocated that, "We should actively construct social and rural systems of housing supply". He also supervised his PhD candidates to study the social system of housing supply.

According to the Report to the Seventeenth National Congress of the Communist Party of China, social construction shall focus on the promotion of livelihood. Accordingly, Wu Liangyong in 2008 pointed out that: "Housing is an important content of livelihood, we should follow the guideline of building a moderately prosperous society in all respects and a harmonious socialist society, take it as an important responsibility of the government in providing public services to tackle the difficult problem of providing housing for urban families with medium or low level of income, to construct a policy system focusing on setting up a social security system of the supply of housing rented at low and affordable price as soon as possible so as to solve the housing problems for urban families with low income through multiple channels. To meet these basic conditions will ensure social stability and security, healthy development, flourishing in all aspects including culture and sciences in spite of the changing global economy. And this is the only way for us to further emancipate the

---

[1] Note made by Zuo Chuan, November 27, 1997.

mind, to develop technologies and human sciences, to make both urban and rural areas prosperous, and to make all the people enjoy livable human settlements."

A.3.3.3 Determining to be the "People's Architect"

Wu Liangyong is also an educator and, for more than six decades, he has supervised several PhD candidates and master graduates. He himself sets an example to them and tells them to serve the public and to construct a livable environment. At the Orientation Meeting of the Department of Architecture, Tsinghua University, held in September 1982, Wu Liangyong made a speech, "I Want to be the People's Architect". At the opening ceremony of Chongqing Institute of Urban Studies held in 1985, Wu Liangyong pointed out that: "People's cities shall serve the people. This means our construction work, including the cultural construction, shall serve the people so that they'll have a better life." Wu Liangyong made a speech during the meeting commemorating the 100th birthday of Liang Sicheng held in 2000. He said: "During the process of accomplishing the great historical mission in the field of architecture, we should learn from the older generation, loving our homeland and the people, working hard for the welfare of the people. I always believe that to love one's homeland and to serve the people are the most basic qualities. Regardless of the trend of globalization in the world, no matter what, we should determine to serve the country and the people. This is the most fundamental responsibility of an architect in China. Therefore, we should advocate developing architecture in the entire society and science of human settlements. As for this, I want to quote what Liang Sicheng said, although it's far away, you won't reach there without walking; although it's a small thing, you won't accomplish it without doing. And this is the great yet practical significance why we should learn from Liang Sicheng." Asian Architects praised Wu Liangyong as the "people's architect".

A.3.4 Cultural Infiltration

Wu Liangyong studied at the National Central University (Chongqing) in 1940 and has worked at Tsinghua University since 1946. He visited other countries to study, learning from many famous masters and following the examples of the older generation in reading extensively and studying both Chinese and foreign theories, finally becoming a learned scholar with a passion to contribute to the society. He adopted a cultural (aesthetic and artistic) perspective in studies of human settlements on the basis of cultural background, proposing theories with profound cultural connotation and characteristics.

Wu Liangyong (2003b) pointed out at a speech delivered at the Graduate School of Chinese Academy of Sciences that, the science of human settlement shall not lose the human spirit; scientific technologies shall combine with human sciences. He also cited actual practice (Ju'er Hutong Project in Beijing) to explain how to apply and promote Chinese culture in architectural designing and city planning.

A.3.4.1   Mountains, Waters, Cities

During the process of urban development, China has always emphasized the combination of natural environment with carefully organized man-made environment. Many traditional cities in China follow the pattern of integrating actual natural conditions of mountains and waters. In terms of theories, every city wants to develop; while in an area, the relationship among mountains, waters, and cities shall be maintained in certain degree, which is another important principle in designing human settlements. Since the 1980s, Wu Liangyong has conducted an analysis on the pattern of mountains, waters, and cities in such cities as Xiamen, Guilin, Sanya, and Wuxi.

Wu Liangyong went to Xiamen for an on-site investigation in April 1984, concluding that Xiamen is a "city surrounded by the sea" with multiple layers of spatial development and the distant view is a city cluster "centering on one city", that the Xiamen island shall be developed by different districts so as to achieve the general pattern of "green areas dotted with buildings, towns, and cities"(Wu Liangyong, 1984b). At the meeting of evaluating the detailed city planning of Guilin held on January 14, 1987, Wu Liangyong summarized that the city of Guilin had distinct features as a landscape city, that is, a city with both mountains and waters, combining the beauty of the city and nature, natural views and cultural views. Facing the challenges of urbanization, he suggested that the construction of the landscape city shall be guided and controlled on a regional perspective so as to integrate micro- and macro-management of the actual construction. The core principles of achieving these include: to maintain the integrity of mountains, waters, and cities (towns and villages), to control the height of buildings, and to emphasize regional human characteristics. In January 1991, under the leadership of Wu Liangyong, the Institute of Architecture & Urban Studies at the Tsinghua University finished the "Research Report on City Planning of the Downtown Area in Sanya City", concluding that the city falls into the category of landscape city integrating mountains, sea, rivers, and the city, recommending that the city planners shall make full use of mountains, the sea, and the rivers as the artistic framework for overall city planning so as to present the features of elegant views of the mountains, the waters, and the city at the same time (Wu Liangyong, et al., 1993). In 1994, Wu Liangyong pointed out at the meeting on studies of overall city planning of Wuxi city that: Wuxi enjoys excellent natural conditions of mountains and waters, which makes the city a perfect candidate for building a landscape city (Wu Liangyong, 1994a). In February 1995, Wu Liangyong visited the Wuxi Institute of City Planning and proposed to build Wuxi into a landscape city.❶ In 2000, on the basis of the architectural artistic planning shown in a Fuzhou map drawn during the Qing Dynasty, which he had collected, Wu Liangyong studied the natural environment of mountains and waters as well as the construction of the city in Fuzhou from the perspective of city planning, including the utilization of mountain and water areas, the location of key architectural complex, the construction of city wall and city gate towers, the arrangement of central axis and alleys, as well as the green areas and suburban scenic sites (Wu Liangyong, 2000a). In view of the analysis made on these cities, Wu Liangyong summarized a concise visual spatial structure diagram on the basis of natural structure, which is a summary made with a profound cultural background, showing his mastery of both traditional city planning skills and local natural characteristics. This makes his practice completely different from the conventional pattern of a "formalistic" structural pattern.

---

❶ Wu Liangyong, "Several Suggestions on Constructing Wuxi as a Landscape City" , *Embracing the New Century: Collection of Works by Wu Liangyong on Urban Studies*, China Architecture and Building Press, 1996.

In a letter to Wu Liangyong dated July 31, 1990, Qian Xuesen clearly proposed the concept of "landscape city". At the seminar on "landscape city" held on February 27, 1993, Wu Liangyong pointed out that the core of "landscape city" was how to handle the relationship between city and the nature. "Landscape city" advocates a harmonious development of man-made and natural environments, aiming to achieve human settlements integrating man-made environment (cities) and natural environment (mountains and waters) (Wu Liangyong, 1993). Wu Liangyong pointed out in a written speech submitted to the Guangzhou Seminar on Landscape City Construction held in 2001 and jointly organized by the Chinese Society for Urban Studies and Nanfang Daily Press Group that "landscape city" is a city pattern integrating mountains, waters, and the city, which emphasizes the functions of mountain and water in city form as well as the cultural connotation of a city (Wu Liangyong, 2001c).

A.3.4.2   City Designing and Culture-Oriented Architectural Designing

Due to a series of changes that occurred during the last decade of the 20th Century, the science of architecture has faced new needs and new opportunities, which expands the scope of architecture and requires more creative thinking patterns as well as reforms in the operation and organization methods of designing work. Wu Liangyong called the changes the turning of human settlements science in direction and started to explore new ways of city designing and culture-oriented architectural designing. For example, Wu Liangyong was in charge of designing the first phase of the Institute of Confucian Studies project in Qufu, Shandong Province, in 1999. On the one hand, he promoted Confucian culture by re-explaining Confucian theories so as to make them function more effectively in modern society; on the other hand, he absorbed the essence of Confucian theories and traditional culture and took them as the source for his designing and inspiration (what Wu Liangyong called as the "motives"). In this project, he managed to promote traditional Chinese architectural culture through such methods of "abstracting and inheriting". In summarizing the experience of designing the first-phase project, Wu Liangyong emphasized the exploration of traditional Chinese culture, the integration of the western architectural theories, the creation of new architectural culture, and the promotion of beauty in traditional Chinese painting rolls. ❶ Accordingly, he supervised several master graduates in the studies in the field, producing theses such as "A Theoretical Study on Regional Architectural Creation: An Insight on the Design of Institute of Confucian Studies in Qufu" (Ni Feng, 1999), and "An Environmental Aesthetic Concept Based on Traditional Chinese Human Philosophy" (Wang Huanyu, 2000). In addition, the designing of the new campus of the China Central Academy of Fine Arts, Nantong Museum, Taishan Museum, and Nanjing Jiangning Weaving and Fabric Manufacturing House also illustrate the exploration along this path. These construction projects integrate natural conditions, city planning, and city spatial designing, combining different arts of architecture, industrial arts, classical gardens, and even rock inscription, containing rich cultural elements, enriching the image of the city.

A.3.4.3   Heritage, Transformation, and Innovation of Regional Culture

"A specific place nurtures local people". With the general background of globalization, urbanization, and modernization, the theories on human settlements initiated by Wu Liangyong pay special attention to the heritage, transformation, and innovation of regional culture and regional planning.

Wu Liangyong (2002b, 2002c, 1989) emphasized on many occasions that: "during the progress of globalization, we study and absorb advanced technologies in creating excellent global culture, while at the same time, we should also be aware of our own cultures, that's an attitude of cultural dignity and the spirit of promoting our own culture." During the process of forming his theories on human settlements, he wrote a series of articles discussing the theme mentioned above, including "On Architectural Culture in Areas to the South of Yangtze River", "Theories on Regional Culture as Shown in Architectural Culture in Areas to the South of Yangtze River", "On Architectural Culture and Regional Architecture", "Basic Concepts, Regional Culture, Time Pattern: Exploring the Path of Architectural Development in China" (Wu Liangyong, 2002b), and "On Studies and Innovations of Architectural Culture in

---

❶ Wu Liangyong, "An Academic Report on the Design of the Institute of Confucian Studies in Qufu", the speech delivered at the Seminar on the Designing of the Institute of Confucian Studies in Qufu, *Architectural Journal*, Issue 7, 2000.

China" (Wu Liangyong, 2002c).

In view of the planning and construction of specific famous historical cities, Wu Liangyong believes that: it is not sufficient to just protect the existing heritages; we should also combine the integral protection of historical areas and historical buildings as well as the construction of new settlements, to construct and innovate along with the protection. We should study the properties of traditional regional cultures so as to find architectural cultural "genes" from the tradition that will nurture current culture, so as to apply them in the current economic and cultural background and to develop them in the construction of new human settlements in a creative way.

A.3.4.4   Learning from Western Cultures

Wu Liangyong usually quotes the following words of Wang Guowei: "As for Chinese and western studies, they will flourish at the same time and decline at the same time too. When the time is right, they will promote each other greatly. In the world today and in view of the studies today, it's impossible that Chinese studies flourish without the flourishing of western studies, or vice versa."[1] He argues that Chinese and western studies are mutually dependant and will promote each other. In order to contribute to their homeland and to the world architectural culture, Chinese scholars must focus on both Chinese and western studies. Accordingly, in order to develop the theories on human settlement, we should also learn from the excellent cultural results in the west.

The comprehensive studies on human settlements made by Wu Liangyong are closely related to his experience of studying with the supervision of Saarinen, for the two of them share the same sources and similar understanding on the concept of designing.[2] Furthermore, his theories on the science of human settlements have been influenced by Greek scholar C. A. Doxiadis and his theories on Ekistics. Wu Liangyong supervised some of his master graduates to systematically study the theories of Doxiadis later (Zhang Xiaoming, 1986) and actively participated in the activities

---

[1]   Refer to *Second Collection of Works by Guantang* (Wang Guowei) (Preface to *Journal of Chinese Studies*).

[2]   Alexander Toniza, "A General Theory of Architecture: Architecture of Realism: A Foreword to the *UIA Beijing Charter, Future of Architecture* by Professor Wu Liangyong", Tsinghua University Press, 2002.

launched by the World Society of Ekistics, acting as its chairman from 1993 to 1995. In addition, Mountfort and his theories on nature and people as well as Kishine Takuro and his theories on integrated urban and rural systematic designing also enriched and helped to develop the science of human settlements initiated by Wu Liangyong.

A.3.4.5 Chinese Spirit of Modernity

Wu Liangyong focused on the realities and problems in China to gradually explore the unknown fields before reaching an initial conclusion of seeking a road of scientific research with distinct Chinese characteristics. During this process, he managed to explore the infinite traditional Chinese cultural treasure, to integrate the western theories and precious experience, and to fully represent the local customs and cultures with distinct Chinese style. Just as Saarinen, his teacher at Cranbrook Academy of Arts, said: "He infused the Chinese spirit of modernity into his work, a spirit coming from not only general development of human culture but also actual growth of life in China. It's a spirit combining the old and the new on the basis of resolution in this country."

In terms of academic development, being directly affected by Liang Sicheng, Lin Huiyin, and Saarinen, Wu Liangyong managed to seek a way to combine technologies and human science, science and art, and to handle the relationship between China and the west, between past and today, finding a way featuring Chinese characteristics and innovation. To acknowledge his long-term efforts of exploration, the International Cultural Council issued in 1989 an Honorary Certificate praising him for his "outstanding work in arts and valuable contributions to human art heritages".

A.4 Methodology Sciences of Human Settlements

For scientific professionals, to improve scientific methodologies is of vital importance. In 1940s, receiving the teachings of Saarinen on the method of thinking, Wu Liangyong returned to China and studied philosophy to get a better understanding on academic theories. For his theories on human settlement, Wu Liangyong greatly emphasized scientific methodologies with holism as the core.

A.4.1　On Holism of Human Settlements

The scientific outlook of Wu Liangyong's science of human settlements is holism. He argues that: "The science of human settlements studying architecture, city, and even region shall be taken as a science on the whole and on holism." "The core of the science of human settlements is to look for inner relationship with the approach of holism, which is also the methodology of the science and its essence"(Wu Liangyong, 2001a). Wu Liangyong follows the principles of cross-disciplinary, comprehensive, and integral studies and his theories on holism of human settlements combine the essence of traditional Chinese culture and the research results of modern sciences.

A.4.1.1　On Holism of Physical Environments

Wu Liangyong's theories on human settlements emphasize the holism of physical environments (from buildings to regions and even the entire world). He has discussed the holism of regional architecture, city, and urban and rural areas for several times. In his "On Paintings by Wu Liangyong" (2002d), he pointed out that: "In view of fine arts, sculpture, architecture, landscape, as well as city planning and regional culture, they all seek aesthetic integrity and holism." In his article "On Architectural Culture and Regional Architecture in Areas to South of Yangtze River", Wu Liangyong pointed out that: "No matter in past, today, or in future, the architectural culture in areas to south of Yangtze River shall integrate the region, cities, architectural complex, individual buildings, as well as the details of each building; it shall be an organic combination of economy, technology, culture, art, and the nature ."❶

A.4.1.2　Inspiration of Traditional Chinese Philosophy

Traditional Chinese philosophy emphasizes integral thinking. Ji Xianlin said: "Oriental philosophical thinking emphasizes synthesis, that is, the concept of holism and of universal connection, advocating comprehensive consideration of an issue." Wu Liangyong holds that the conclusion is concise and of significant importance to

---

❶ Wu Liangyong, "Architectural Culture in Areas to the South of Yangtze River and Regional Architecture" , *Embracing the New Century*: *Collection of Works by Wu Liangyong on Urban Studies*, China Architecture and Building Press, 1996.

understanding the science of human settlements. The systematic and integral thinking on human settlement can be rooted in the profound traditional Chinese philosophical theories with a long history. For example, Wu Liangyong was in charge of the drafting of UIA Beijing Charter, and he derived inspiration from the ancient philosophy of "different people have different opinions on the same issues, but they will reach the same goal by different routes", concluding that: firstly, in the world of diversity, we should operate from a strategically advantageous position in finding the spirit of integration. Ancient Chinese philosophies emphasize holistic thinking as well as comprehensive integration, and the thinking pattern of synthesizing on the basis of analysis has become the essence treasured by all people as well as the compass for us to handle complicated actual situations and problems. Secondly, a common goal can be achieved through different ways. Since different regions have different conditions, the architectural development in different regions and countries must follow different ways in accordance with their specific conditions. At the same time, all people in the world cherish the one common goal of realizing a happy life and sustainable development. In this way, the science of human settlements and the oriental philosophies help to solve the academic problems and puzzles in this century, exploring the general development trend in the new century (Wu Liangyong, 2003d). The Beijing Charter shows clearly that Wu Liangyong applied the systematic and holistic Chinese philosophical wisdom, expanding the study objective of architecture from buildings to human settlements, setting up the disciplinary cluster for the science of human settlements, creating its theoretical framework and knowledge system, integrating separate majors in architecture with a higher level study subject, exploring the ways to solve difficult issues in the new century.

A.4.1.3　The Concept of Holism in a System of Complexity

In the 1980s, some foreign scholars proposed the issue of science of complexity, studying the open and complicated mega system, which is a new direction of the modern scientific thinking pattern. Human settlement is a complicated mega system including architecture, village, town, and region. During the process of its development and facing complicated natural and social issues, it requires the methodology of the science of complexity. On the basis of the existing research results on complexity, Wu Liangyong further explored some theoretical methods concerning the science of human settlements in his "Introduction to Human Settlement Science": (1) the interrelation of different sciences; (2) the science of integration and holism; and (3) the open and complicated mega system (Wu Liangyong, 2001a). He applied the concepts of the science of complexity to direct the studies on human settlement planning in northwest Yunnan Province and supervised his master graduate on the "Studies on Methodology of Human Settlement Science Based on Complexity Science" (Yu Haiyi, 2001). At the 201st Seminar on Scientific Issues Concerning Urban Development in China held in April 2003, Wu Liangyong pointed out that: "Urban studies shall be based on holism with the help of the science of complexity and non-linear thinking to promote their development."

A.4.2 Comprehensive and Integrated Studies

The science of human settlement is a disciplinary cluster centering on urban and rural development as well as relevant issues. Its goal is to explore a cross- and multi-discipline cluster through theoretical research and actual construction practice to integrate natural sciences, technological sciences, human sciences, arts, and other studies concerning human settlements, so as to create a new scientific system. Through years of studies, Wu Liangyong proposed to develop comprehensive and integrated studies focusing on actual problems, breaking through original disciplinary boundaries and applying relevant research results (Wu Liangyong, 1997c).

A.4.2.1   Coherence-Integrating Methodology

Faced with the extremely complicated human settlement mega system, the science of human settlements manages to coordinate and control the construction of human settlements; accordingly, the studies on the science of human settlements shall be conducted on a comprehensive basis of integration and synthesis (cross-disciplinary research). At the pre-research approval and appraisal meeting on studies of sustainable development planning of human settlements in northwest Yunnan Province held in August 1999, Wu Liangyong clearly pointed out that: "The so-called integration is to synthesize all relevant subjects to find problems for problem-oriented solutions, and then to synthesize further on this basis. This is the methodology of meta synthesis." The research framework producing the final research report is the product of this meta synthesis (Wu Liangyong, 2000d). In his "Introduction to Human Settlement Science" published in 2001, Wu Liangyong proposed "to grasp the parts of peripheral subjects in relevance to architecture (please note the restriction of relevant parts) before digesting them (have a profound understanding on them). In order to emphasize the feature of meta synthesis of the work, I call it the coherence-integrating methodology." Jin Wulun (2007a) believes that in view of comprehensive cross- and multi-disciplinary perspective, the methodology of the science of human settlement is coherence-integrating.

A.4.2.2   Being "Extensive" yet "Focusing"

Facing the extremely complicated issues, Wu Liangyong argues that the research approach should be "extensive" and "focusing". To be "extensive" means to study the issues from a broad perspective so as to handle the complexity of human settlements; while to be "focusing" means to grasp the main points instead of being trapped by the philosophy of complexity. To be more specific, with regard to some minor issues, no thorough and complete understanding is required; but for key issues, thorough studies are the must so as to gain a complete understanding of the issue. This is a hard task of study and the scholars must try their best to achieve it (Wu Liangyong, 2003c). The theories and methodology of studying human settlement are no simple adding of existing knowledge, but the mastering of the open and complicated mega system or, in the words of Qian Xuesen, a process developing "from complexity to simplicity" so as to have a "bird's view on the whole picture"(Wu Liangyong, 2001a). Wu Liangyong (2008) holds that the science of human settlements shall be nurtured by multiple disciplines and take all specialized relevant contents of these disciplines as "common knowledge" and "ordinary truths" so that they would be easily understood and accepted by the society and become the common goal of the entire society. Scientific researchers shall share the same goals and destiny with the public so as to motivate the entire society to achieve the established goals.

A.4.2.3   Scientific Community

In order to conduct integrating and comprehensive studies on human settlements, Wu Liangyong managed to organize a new organizational framework involving multiple disciplines, the "scientific community". The Studies on the Planning of Sustainable Development of Human Settlements in Northwest Yunnan Province conducted from April 1998 to August 1999 under the leadership of Wu Liangyong involved more than 50 scholars from Tsinghua University and seven other units in Yunnan Province. The project produced two important results, one of which was to organize a multi-disciplinary research team and a research framework and, with joint efforts of the research team and local authorities, form an academic organization and strength on launching multi-disciplinary studies on the protection and development of northwest areas in Yunnan Province, as well as the research framework on the studies of biological diversity, cultural diversity, social and economic development, and the construction of human settlements. From 1999 to 2001, Wu Liangyong was in charge of the studies on the Planning of Urban and Rural Spatial Development in the Beijing-Tianjin-North Hebei Province Region (the Greater Beijing Region), involving several hundreds of scholars from a dozen different organizations. Relevant authorities and different research institutes in Beijing, Tianjin, and Hebei Province cooperated in the study project and established a "scientific community", communicating and exchanging at different levels, applying the scientific theories on human settlements at regional levels in a creative way to solve actual problems. From 2005 to 2007, Wu Liangyong was in charge of "Engineering Environment Planning on South-to-North Water Diversion Central Trunk Line Project" and, with the guidance of the scientific outlook on development, gathered over one hundred scholars from different fields of planning, architecture, landscape, water conservancy, environment, historical culture, transportation, and digital technologies in compiling the overall plans on architectural environment so as to comprehensively consider water conservancy projects with the nature, economy, society, and culture, to coordinate the development of water source areas, the areas along the project line, and the consuming areas, as well as to harmonize the relations among planning, designing, construction, and management.

A.4.3   On Holistic Designing

Wu Liangyong emphasizes the scientific methodology of holism and has always promoted disciplinary integration and the studies on holism. He pointed out that: "For many years, my work ranged greatly from architectural and city designing to landscape designing to city planning, and even regional studies, but I always start from "holistic design thinking" and learn to analyze, understand, and finally solve problems from philosophical perspective. In view of my specialized activities, I manage to explore the chain of relations among different fields so as to promote my professional activities." (Wu Liangyong, 2004b).

A.4.3.1   Holistic Thinking on the Planning and Designing of Human Settlements

The space of human settlements is continuous and, from the most basic living unit of room to building, architecture complex, community, city, city cluster, and region, all these are interrelated and mutually affected. In certain spatial scope, they form entities at different levels and are interrelated to each other. In his continuous scientific studies and practice, Wu Liangyong has studied points, lines, areas, and regions, finding out their inner relationship and realizing that together they form a big entity and a system.

In his "Introduction to Human Settlement Science", Wu Liangyong proposed that the planning and designing should be guided by the "science of holism" to further integrate planning and designing principles, to make holistic thinking on relevant issues, and to finally construct livable human settlements. The focus of the studies remains being comprehensive and using holistic thinking for the spatial relationships, forms, and quality of human settlements, so as to gradually realize: (1) the integrated economic development by promoting urban and rural economic growth, regional cooperation, and the integration of economic network; (2) the integrated regional space by promoting the integration of large cities, mega cities, middle, and small cities in certain areas, reinforcing planning and overall arrangement with the condition of limited space so as to make reasonable use of land resources on an economical basis; (3) the integrated urban and rural development by coordinating urban and rural construction, developing agriculture, forestry, and livestock industry in the areas as well as protecting natural ecological environment in the area; (4) the integrated development stages by combining short-term and long-term goals established on an open system.

A.4.3.2　Different Focuses at Different Spatial Levels

Wu Liangyong proposed that, according to the changes of overall architectural, urban, and regional scale and at specific planning level, we should take all relevant elements into comprehensive consideration so as to unify personal expression with overall coordination. Sure enough, there should be different focuses in planning and designing as well as: (1) the concept of regional block, to explore such urban development patterns as "region-city theories", "regional architecture theories", and "landscape theories" so as to development from gardens to landscape (such as the proposal on the Quehua National Park in Jinan); (2) the concept of "city unit", to base the designing and planning on the theories of overall city planning, to coordinate among infrastructure facilities, and to regulate city texture and order; (3) the exploration of cultural connotation, to mold the modern architectural soul by integrating fine arts, architecture, sculpture, calligraphy, industrial arts, and by promoting cultural content of the environment.

A.4.3.3　Going Beyond Reductionism

Wu Liangyong has participated in the designing of human settlements covering different fields of studies on architecture, city, landscape, and region, creating a big platform for the comprehensive and multi-disciplinary studies, achieving great results in cross-disciplinary practice, which makes him an outstanding representative in the field of multi-disciplinary practice. At the National Architectural Education Direction Committee Meeting held on September 14, 2007, Wu Liangyong delivered a speech on philosophical thinking on the reform of architectural education, advocating "developing holism and going beyond reductionism". He believes that "in order to have a better understanding on something, you'd better study it in a holistic way. To find out the inter-relationship among its different aspects as well as the way how these aspects restricting each other, that's the only way to master the main principle of designing." "Today, our construction activities have improved greatly, accordingly, our architectural perspective expands greatly to cover both the urban and rural areas in all four directions. The architecture is closely related to geographical, social, economic, and cultural development, which requires us to adopt a holistic thinking pattern more earnestly than ever to explore the future of architecture. Different people might have different understandings on the whole picture, yet all will agree on its importance, which goes beyond the concept of holistic space of designing we discuss today."[1]

A.4.3.4 Theories on Development and Generation

Theories on generation form an important content of traditional Chinese philosophy and discuss the generation and evolution process of things. "The theories on human settlement designing held by Wu Liangyong propose a unique way to solve problems from the generation mechanism and fall into the category of holistic generative holism methodology"(Jin, Wulun, 1994, 2000, 2006, 2007b). Generative methodology is a methodology of process, which introduces the real time in the studies and enables combining the way of understanding things with actual practice. In his "Introduction to Human Settlement Science", Wu Liangyong proposed that: "the time is always changing and we need a scientific attitude, meticulous thinking, rich imagination to study the process of the system of complexity by following objective rules, to consider the actual situation and to adroitly guide action according to circumstances, to plan, design, and operate our changing settlements with dynamic perspectives and methods." In other words, the theories on designing the time and space of human settlements integrate "time, space, and the world" while emphasizing a harmonious and orderly integration.

---

[1] Wu Liangyong, "Developing Holism and Exceeding Reductionism: Some Philosophical Thoughts on the Reform of Architecture Education" , the speech delivered at Guidance Commission National Meeting on Architecture Education held at the China Central Academy of Fine Arts, September 14, 2007.

In view of the methodology of human settlement science, Wu Liangyong is full of wisdom by emphasizing coordination, integration and harmony, which is the general development of modern sciences and the soul and core of the scientific theories on human settlements held by Wu Liangyong. This is the strength of his theories.

A.5 Conclusion

For more than a half of the century and especially since China adopted policies of reform and opening-up, facing the urgent needs of national and social development, Wu Liangyong has adopted a broad perspective in studying both Chinese and western theories and absorbing the essence of previous research results in proposing his own theories on the science of human settlements. Wu Liangyong started from the small aspects that people are used to and developed a new direction for academic studies with a visionary spirit of the time, having an influence on a generation of scholars. Through synthetic and comprehensive studies and overall designing, Wu Liangyong explored the general issues of human settlements and possible solutions. From historical a perspective, this is an important stage of his academic life or a new level. On a comparative perspective, the theories on human settlements held by Wu Liangyong have such characteristics of serving the society and the public, environmental designing, caring for people, and culture infiltration.

Since the theories on human settlements are closely related to national economy and livelihood of the people, once they have taken shape, they would be extensively accepted by the society. Today, his proposal of "'creating a better human settlement" has become common in the entire society and accepted by the state authorities, which greatly improves the status of urban and rural construction in national economy and produces great social and economic efficiency.

Jin Wulun summarizes that the ultimate goals of the science of human settlements are "to make everyone have a place to live in, to make every house suitable to its environment, to beautify the habitat and to improve the livelihood of people, and to realize harmonious development of the entire society," which are in accordance with the traditional Confucian principles of "achieving the perfect virtue and the perfect path and realizing the established goals". Wu Liangyong likes to quote a famous saying by Zhang Zai, a Chinese philosopher who lived during the Song Dynasty (960-1279) to express his passion for academic studies and his life-long goal, with which this article will conclude as well: "to establish a mind for heaven and earth, to decide the ultimate meaning of life for people, to inherit the most valuable learning of the past sages, and to pave the way for the forever peace."

Since the science of human settlement is a developing frontier subject, there is still a long way to go to gain a better understanding for professional scholars, the society, and for decision makers. We look forward to stepping out of the status of chaos and to achieve gradually common understanding in the academic community, the entire society, and among decision makers, so as to gradually promote the science of human settlements to a higher level. We also expect that, along with social evolution, more and more people will devote to the studies of human settlement science to continuously improve it to higher levels.

Bibliography

[1] Chen Weibang, "Professor Wu Liangyong and Urban Studies in China", City Planning Review, Issue 7, 2002.

[2] He Xinghua, "Dilemma of and Solution to Positive Science in City Planning" (PhD Dissertation), Tsinghua University, 2007.

[3] Huang He, "Cultural Planning: An Approach Promoting Comprehensive City Development by Using Cultural Resources" (PhD Dissertation), Tsinghua University, 2005.

[4] Huo Bing, "Theories and Practice of Strategic Spatial Planning in China: A Case Study of Tianjin and Beijing-Tianjin-Hebei Area" (PhD Dissertation), Tsinghua University, 2006.

[5] Jin Wulun, "Methodology of Human Settlement Science", teaching material on the introduction of human settlement science in Tsinghua University, December 2007a.

[6] Jin Wulun, "Concept of Generation in Complex Adaptive System", Jianghan Forum, Issue 8, 2007b.

[7] Jin Wulun, "From System Holism to Generation Holism", Science Times, November 30, 2006.

[8] Jin Wulun, Generation Philosophy, Hebei University Press, 2000.

[9] Jin Wulun, "Introduction to Generation Philosophy", Natural Philosophy (Vol. 1), ed. by Wu Guosheng, China Social Science Press, 1994.

[10] Liu Jian, "Suburban Development Based on Regional Integration: What shall Rapidly Urbanized Beijing Learn from Paris" (PhD Dissertation), Tsinghua University, 2003.

[11] Mao Qizhi, "From General Architecture to Human Settlement Science: An Interview of Wu Liangyong, Academician of Chinese Academy of Science and Chinese Academy of Engineering, and Professor of Tsinghua University", The Construction of Changjiang, Issue 3, 2000.

[12] Ni Feng, "A Theoretical Study on Regional Architectural Creation: An Insight on the Design of Institute of Confucian Studies in Qufu" (Master Thesis), Tsinghua University, 1999.

[13] Ou Xiaokun, "Ecological Security and Human Settlement: A Case Study on Northwest Yunnan Province" (PhD Dissertation), Tsinghua University, 2006.

[14] Shan Jixiang, "The Protection of Cultural Heritage and the Construction of City Culture" (PhD Dissertation), Tsinghua University, 2008.

[15] Shan Jun, "Regional Features of Architecture and Cities: A Study on Regional Architecture Based on Human Settlement Concepts" (PhD Dissertation), Tsinghua University, 2002.

[16] Song Qilin, "Gathering Creative Thoughts, Revealing Dedication to Studies: Reflection on Reading Architecture, City, Human Settlement by Wu Liangyong", Huazhong Architecture, Issue 2, 2004.

[17] Tan Qinglian, "Dedicating to the Great Career of Improving Human Settlement Environment", Architectural Journal, Issue 8, 1990.

[18] Wang Guangtao, "An Intensive Study on How to Improve Urban and Rural Planning", City Planning Review, Issue 11, 2004.

[19] Wang Huanyu, "An Environmental Aesthetic Concept Based on Traditional Chinese Human Philosophy" (Master Thesis), Tsinghua University, 2000.

[20] Wu Liangyong, "Introduction to Human Settlement Science", China Architecture and Building Press, 2001a.

[21] Wu Liangyong, "Preface to Complete Works by Liang Sicheng", China Architecture and Building Press, 2001b.

[22] Wu Liangyong, "On Landscape City", Urban Studies, Issue 2, 2001c.

[23] Wu Liangyong, "Exploring Distinct Beauty of a City", Urban and Rural Development, Issue 1, 2002a.

[24] Wu Liangyong, "Basic Concepts, Regional Culture, Time Pattern: Exploring the Path of Architectural Development in China", Architectural Journal, Issue 2, 2002b.

[25] Wu Liangyong, "On Studies and Innovations of Architectural Culture in China" (Preface 1 to Research Library of Chinese Architectural Culture), Huazhong Architecture, Issue 6, 2002c.

[26] Wu Liangyong, "On Paintings by Wu Liangyong", SDX Joint Publishing Company, 2002d.

[27] Wu Liangyong, "On Historical Task of Studying and Innovating Chinese Architectural Culture", City Planning Review, Issue 1, 2003a.

[28] Wu Liangyong, "Human Reflections on Human Settlement Science", Urban Studies, Issue 5,

2003b.

[29] Wu Liangyong, Architecture, City, and Human Settlement, Series by Chinese Academicians, Hebei Education Press, 2003c.

[30] Wu Liangyong, "Entering a New Era of Human Habitat Progress", Architecture, City, and Human Settlement, Series by Chinese Academicians, Hebei Education Press, 2003d.

[31] Wu Liangyong, "Education on Human Settlement Science and Landscape Science", Chinese Landscape Architecture, Issue 1, 2004a.

[32] Wu Liangyong, "Technology, Human Science, and Architecture: Personal Thoughts on Dedicating to Human Settlement Science", China University Teaching, Issue 1, 2004b.

[33] Wu Liangyong, "The Most Intense Conflicts and the Best Opportunities: Expectations on Architectural Development in China", Engineering Science, Issue 2, 2004c.

[34] Wu Liangyong, "New Development Concepts and Human Settlement Science: the Speech in Written Form at the First International Habitat Festival Held in Weihai", Development of Small Cities and Towns, Issue 9, 2004d.

[35] Wu Liangyong, "Systematic Analysis and Integral Strategy: Human Settlement Science and New Development Concepts", City Planning Review, Issue 2, 2005a.

[36] Wu Liangyong, "Promoting the Development of Planning with Urban Studies and Practice, a Speech Delivered at the Annual Meeting of City Planning Held in 2004", City Planning Review, Issue 4, 2005b.

[37] Wu Liangyong, "Regional Planning and Human Settlement Construction", Urban Studies, Issue 4, 2005c.

[38] Wu Liangyong, "Constructing Splendid Landscape with the Help of Famous Paintings: A Tentative Discussion on Quehua Historical and Cultural Park in Jinan", Chinese Landscape Architecture, Issue 1, 2006.

[39] Wu Liangyong, "The Protection of Cultural Heritage and the Construction of Cultural Environment: for Chinese Culture Heritage Day on 9 June 2007", City Planning Review, Issue 8, 2007.

[40] Wu Liangyong, "The Transition of Development Pattern and the Exploration of Human Settlement Science", 2007 Chinese City Development Report, ed. by China Mayor Association, China City Press, 2008.

[41] Wu Liangyong, et. al., "Exploring the City Designing of Sanya Downtown Area", City Planning Review, Issue 2, 1993.

[42] Wu Liangyong, and his research team, "Suggestions on Emphasizing Integral and Systematic Regional Development in Developed Areas", China Construction News, 19 May 1998.

[43] Wu Liangyong, et. al., Zhang Jian and First City of Nantong in Modern China, China Architecture and Building Press, 2006a.

[44] Wu Liangyong, et. al, Studies on Urban and Rural Spatial Development Planning in Beijing-

Tianjin-Hebei Area (Second-Phase Report), Tsinghua University Press, 2006b.

[45] Wu Liangyong, et. al, "Engineering Environment Planning on South-to-North Water Diversion Central Trunk Line Project", Tsinghua University, March 2007.

[46] Wu Liangyong, Zhao Wanmin, "The Three Gorges Project and the Construction of Human Settlement", City Planning Review, Issue 4, 1995.

[47] Wu Liangyong, Zhao Wanmin, "Studies on the Three Gorges Project and the Construction of Human Settlement", Frontiers of Science and Technology in China, Chinese Academy of Engineering, 1997.

[48] Wu Liangyong, Zhou Ganzhi, Lin Zhiqun, "Today and Tomorrow of China Construction Industry", China City Press, 1994.

[49] Yu Haiyi, "Studies on Methodology of Human Settlement Science Based on Complexity Science" (Master Thesis), Tsinghua University, 2001.

[50] Yu Haiyi, "A Tentative Study on the History of Modern City Planning and Construction in Nantong and on Zhang Jian's Theories on City Planning"(PhD Dissertation), Tsinghua University, 2005.

[51] Zhai Hui, "Shangrila, Utopia, and Ideal City: A Study on Human Settlement in Shangrila Area" (PhD Dissertation), Tsinghua University, 2005.

[52] Zhang Xiaoming, "Commentary Review on Doxiadis and Human Settlement Science" (Master Thesis), Tsinghua University, 1986.

[53] Zhang Yue, "On the Forms and Construction of Human Settlement in Haidai Area before Qin Dynasty" (PhD Dissertation), Tsinghua University, 2003.

[54] Zhao Liang, "On Spatial Development of the Corridor Area in Beijing and Tianjin: Its History, Present, and Future" (PhD Dissertation), Tsinghua University, 2006.

[55] Zhao Wanmin, "Studies on the Three Gorges Project and the Construction of Human Settlement" (PhD Dissertation), Tsinghua University, 1996.

[56] CAS Department of Science and Technology, "Today and Tomorrow of Construction Industry in China (Abstract)", Bulletin of the Chinese Academy of Science, Issue 2, 1994.

[57] Zhou Ganzhi, "On Professor Wu Liangyong and Human Settlement Science", City Planning Review, Issue 7, 2002.

[58] Zhou Ganzhi, "Progressing with the Time and Developing Urban Studies", Urban Studies, Issue 4, 2007.

[59] Zhou Qinghua, "The Treatment of Loess Plateau Area in North Shaanxi Province and the Applicable Pattern for Spatial Form Evolution of Human Settlement" (PhD Dissertation), Tsinghua University, 2006.

Wu Liangyong:
A Great Conductor of
"Symphony for Concrete"

By WEN Aiping

From ancient times to the present, Jiangnan (the region south of the Yangtze River) has been the breeding ground for great talents. While visitors are enchanted by the flamboyance of the decorated boats paddled down the Qinhuai River amidst lantern lights and music played on flutes and drums, countless refined scholars and artists have emerged from this very place. Mr. Wu Liangyong, Professor at Tsinghua University, and academician of the Chinese Academy of Sciences and Chinese Academy of Engineering is among the talents who have made their way to success from this land of the gifted.

My interview was postponed several times because of Professor Wu's fully tight schedule. Today even in his 80s, he is still working hard for the cause of architecture and urban planning in China. Are there any other reasons for that besides his vitality? When the interview was finally carried out, his brief opening remarks enlightened me.

"There are not many romantic stories in my life. In my childhood when the country was blighted by the tragedy of the Japanese intrusion, I had to leave home in order to evade the war. This experience gives me a deep understanding about the suffering of the Chinese race and makes me realize the responsibilities and duties of an educated Chinese. This has kept me going till today."

WU Liangyong was born in Nanjing in May 1922. When he was a little boy, he demonstrated great interests in many things, studying hard and getting excellent results at school. In his adolescence when China suffered the disaster of war, he fled with his family from Nanjing before the occupation of Japanese army and managed his way to Chongqing. The suffering arising from the destruction of his nation and home and drifting from one place to another to evade the war made him determine to take up architecture as a career so as to contribute to the post-war reconstruction. In 1940, he enrolled in the Department of Architecture of Central University and graduated with a Bachelor's degree in engineering in 1944.

In his professional career of more than 60 years, WU Liangyong has made significant contributions to the development of architecture and urban planning in China. As one of the most famous masters of architecture and urban planning in contemporary China, his theoretical and practical achievements are highly appreciated both domestically and overseas. Just a few days before this interview, he received the academician certificate and badge of French Academy of Architecture in Paris. When he showed me the golden badge, I could read through his easy and firm eyes the great efforts that he made for the cause of architecture and urban planning in China for more than half a century. Indeed, many of the projects that he carried out are worth mentioning, particularly those in the last decade or so.

From 1987 to 1992, he presided over the project of New Courtyard House Complex at Ju'er Hutong Neighborhood in the Old City of Beijing, which was awarded the Golden Medal in Architecture of ARCASIA (Architects Regional Council Asia) and the World Habitat Award of the United Nations in 1992. In 1999, he chaired the 20th Congress of UIA (Union of International Architects) in Beijing and drafted the Beijing Charter, an important declaration of international architects at the turn of the new Century. In 2000, he, together with more than 40 academicians and more than 100 architects, wrote to the Central Government of China, appealing for reassessing Paul Andrew's proposal for the National Opera House in Beijing. In 2001, he led the research on the Rural & Urban Spatial Development Planning of Greater Beijing Region. In 2002 he received the Prince Claus Funds Award of the Dutch Government. Since late 2002, he has presided over the research on the Strategies of Spatial Development of Beijing and taken part in the comprehensive planning of Beijing as a leading consultant.

B.1 Teaching Tirelessly by Personal Example as well as Verbal Instruction

Since becoming a faculty member at Tsinghua University, Wu has been completely engaged in architecture education. In 1946 after the anti-Japanese war, he started to work as an assistant to LIANG Si'cheng helping to set up the Department of Architecture at the Tsinghua University. When LIANG Si'cheng went to the US for lectures after the establishment of the department, it was Professor LIN Huiyin and WU Liangyong who took charge of the courses. Thanks to LIANG Si'cheng's recommendation, WU went to the US for an advanced study at Cranbrook Academy of

Art led by Eliel Saarinen, a famous Finnish architect. Two years later when he got his Master's degree, he received a letter from LIANG Si'cheng stating the great demand for construction talents for the development of new China. This prompted him to return to China immediately and to resume his teaching career at the Tsinghua University.

In 1951, Wu wrote an article in the People's Daily, calling for due attention to architecture education and "for training more efficiently and more prolifically the workforce for basic infrastructures". Since then, he has put forward successively constructive proposals concerning architecture education, for example, to expand the scope of architecture and to integrate practical activities with theoretical studies. In particular, he, together with Professor WANG Juyuan at the Agriculture University, set up the course on landscape jointly organized by both universities; and recruited the first batch of students majoring in landscape planning and design at Tsinghua University, which subsequently led to the establishment of the Department of Landscape & Planning in the Beijing Forestry University.

Following the university restructuring in 1952, the Department of Architecture & Engineering of the Engineering School at Beijing University was merged with Tsinghua, which consequently brought about the significant expansion of the Department of Architecture of Tsinghua. As the Deputy Director of the department in charge of both teaching and administration at that time, Wu paid much attention to establishing new teaching systems in accordance with the specific situations of China, the general trends of architectural development, and the successful experiences of other countries. Years later with more staff and students as well as enhanced teaching quality, the Department of Architecture of Tsinghua became one of the most influential centers of architecture education in China.

In the past decades, Wu has continued working hard in the frontier of architecture education. He became the advisor for postgraduate students of architecture in the early 1950s and for PhD candidates in 1981. In 1984, one of his students got the Doctor's degree and became the first Doctor of Urban Planning and Design in China; and thanks to Wu's instruction, his doctoral thesis titled "Planning Research on Beijing Olympic Games and Asian Games" was awarded the First Prize for Scientific & Technical

Advancement by the Education Committee of China. Many of his students are highly acclaimed for the considerable theoretical and practical values of their theses. Since the evaluation system for excellent doctoral thesis was tried out in China in recent years, two of the top three theses were from his students. At present, he still supervises more than 20 PhD and Master's degree candidates.

Since the 1980s, based on his studies on the achievements and failures of architecture education in the west, as well as the experiences and lessons of architecture education in China, Wu has tried his best to establish the system of architecture education in China. His proposals to "set up hierarchical education system and bring up architectural professionals of different kinds", to "integrate education with research and practice", to "highlight the social training of architects", and to "transform the concept of architectural design into that of planning and design of human settlements" are indeed the generalization of the characteristics of Chinese architecture education, as well as the proposition for the development strategies of the building industry. Thanks to his contributions, the Department of Architecture of Tsinghua turned into the School of Architecture in 1988, from which many professionals in architecture, landscape, and urban planning have been nurtured.

His insistence in exploring the Chinese way of architecture education and his significant contributions to the architecture education reform in China are so influential both domestically and overseas that in 1996 Wu was awarded the Jean Tschumi Prize of UIA in recognition of his contributions.

B.2 Chinese Culture as Basis and Western Culture as Reference

If we call western architecture "a history book of stones", Chinese architecture can be regarded is "a history book of wood", which is more difficult to preserve.

Wu initiated his research on the rehabilitation of traditional neighborhoods in the Old City of Beijing in 1978. He advocated the theory of "organic renewal" and proposed that the prototype of "new courtyard house" should be worked out to meet the demand of modern life while respecting the urban context and fabrics of the Old City of Beijing. He argues that a city is a living organ that is always in the process of metabolism. It is impossible to protect a city in the way of protecting a mummy, while it is also unreasonable to renew a city in the way of completely replacing the old with the new. The only possible way is to promote the organic renewal of the city following the principle of metabolism. This encompasses facilitating the "micro-circulation" of the city by eliminating "dead cells", generating "new cells" and revitalizing the cells that are still alive, for example, old buildings can be adapted for other uses. In 1988, thanks to the support of the Beijing Municipal Government, Wu presided over the project of Planning and Design of New Courtyard House Complex at Ju' er Hutong Neighborhood in the Old City of Beijing. Based on his concept of organic renewal, he started the planning and design process by firstly classifying the existing buildings according to their quality and then defining different development strategies correspondingly. Buildings in good quality, especially those constructed after the 1970s, would be preserved. A number of old courtyard houses in relatively good conditions would be rehabilitated while some dilapidated buildings would be demolished and replaced by new ones. All the new buildings were of two or three stories, following the prototype of New Courtyard House. From the viewpoint of urban design, they became organic parts of the spatial system of hutong-courtyard of the Old City of Beijing, leaving the courtyards as the node of the neighborhood structure and the public space for community life. From the viewpoint of architecture, they integrated the advantages of modern apartment buildings and traditional courtyard houses, keeping more private spaces for family members to meet the demand of modern life.

Wu's achievements in the Ju'er Hutong project are greatly appreciated in the field of architecture both domestically and overseas. This experimental project was awarded the First Prize for Excellent Architectural Design of Beijing Municipal Government in 1991 and the Golden Medal in Architecture of ARCASIA and the World Habitat Award of United Nations in 1992. In 1990, a famous British architectural reviewer argued that the experiences gained during the Ju'er Hutong project could serve as guidance to the urban rehabilitation of the developing countries in Asia. This is also what Wu considered as the final goal of this experimental project. Actually, all of his projects are carried out following a problem-oriented methodology, aiming at resolving the practical problems of Chinese cities. He emphasizes that creation should be done instead of only be discussed and all that he has done in the past two decades has been finding a way of urban planning and urban construction with Chinese characteristics.

After the reforms and the opening-up to the outside world in the 1980s, different theories and schools of architecture poured into China, bringing about significant influences on its urban development. During a period of 20 years, many buildings had been constructed in Chinese cities, yet most of them were deficient in the urban context, leading Chinese cities into the dilemma of "different cities with same appearance". In particular, some Chinese cities became the laboratory of foreign architects for their experiments of unconventional architecture. Many exotic buildings were imported directly from overseas, resulting in great damages to the traditional urban fabrics and urban context of Chinese cities. As a Chinese architect, Wu cannot hold his indignation to this event. "I don't mean that we should not learn from the west, neither should we be against unconventional ideas that are mostly needed in art and culture. Personally, I learn a lot from other countries through my studies and visits overseas, as well as my contacts with foreign architects. Yet, learning from other countries does not mean photocopying their work. Some of their experiences are successful and meaningful, while some are unsuccessful and unworthy. I do not agree to regard something ephemeral as the future of China." At the same time, he is very anxious about the ignorance of Chinese architects of their own culture, such as abandoning the fundamental principles of architecture, disregarding the continuity and development of history, giving up the exploration of traditional Chinese culture. He is quite sad that today Chinese architects do not have enough knowledge about Chinese culture and do not work hard enough on it. "In the light of globalization, we should learn from the excellent cultures of other countries, especially advanced sciences and technologies. Meanwhile, we should keep in our minds the idea of cultural consciousness, the attitude of cultural pride, and the spirit of cultural improvement, so as to create an excellent global culture by the way of integrating the eastern culture with the western one."

Taking his design work on the Confucian Institute at Qufu, Shandong Province, as an example, Wu explained in detail his concerns on traditional Chinese culture.

"Today, many important projects, particularly those concerning cultural activities, are located at crucial sites. Unfortunately, we cannot find necessary cultural connotations from the architectural designs. This makes me very upset. When dealing with the architectural design of the Confucian Institute, we firstly characterized it as a building with special functions (to research and develop Confucianism) and located in a special place (hometown of Confucius). As a contemporary building in a cultural city, it should be a modern architecture full of specific cultural characters. Based on our studies on the architectural culture during the period of Warring States and the architectural evolution of traditional Chinese schools, we made a series of proposals, ranging from site planning to architecture composition as well as the elements of interior and exterior decoration. In order to create the feeling of 'convivial Holy land', we made use of the skills of both Chinese and Western architecture." As a result, this modern building is so unique that it is hailed as a landmark building of the city.

Wu believes that in a country with a long history like China, almost every city and every site could provide architects and urban planners with opportunities to exert their ideas. The stories concerning the history, geography, and culture of the city or the site will bring more inspirations and imaginations to architects or urban planners. It is just like the depictions of great poets such as LI Bai, DU Fu, or SU Dongpo, which will definitely make landscape of mountains and rivers more vivid and attractive. He argues that "architecture is an integration of art and science. Architecture development in the 21st Century calls for not only scientific innovations but also artistic creations. Chinese architects are, relatively speaking, not strong in terms of art pursuits, to which due efforts should be made."

B.3 Sciences of Human Settlements and General Theory of Architecture

Blue sky, green land, clear water, as well as cleanness and serenity are not only the necessary elements of a livable environment, which is the common aspiration of all human beings, but also the fundamental criteria of sustainable development. However, the depletion of resources and the deterioration of the environment in the latter half of the last century have been even greater than that of the entire human history before then. While we enjoy the advantages of human civilization, we have to face the punishments of the nature and pay great costs for our errors. Today, we finally realize that our attitude toward nature should be changed. Creating better human settlements has become an eternal topic of the era.

As the founder of Sciences of Human Settlements in China, Wu argues that the development of sciences today calls for the concept of "macro science". Human settlement is a mega-system of complexity, including buildings, cities, and regions. When dealing with the problems of nature and society occurring in the process of development, the methodology of complex sciences should be adopted so as to analyze and resolve the problems from holistic and interdisciplinary perspectives. For example, in the past we used to think that architecture is confined only to the work of architects. Yet, when urban planning came into existence as a discipline, the social phenomenon of residence also became a part of architecture. Today, cities confronted with many problems should not be dealt with in a piecemeal manner, but be treated holistically from different perspectives, such as settlement, region, culture, science and technology, economy, art, policy, legislation, education, and even philosophy. Based on the traditional concept of architecture, a general theory of architecture should be established to solve the complex problems of human settlements.

As an architect, Wu's lifelong goals are to create better human settlements in harmony with nature and to make people live poetically on earth, which are his personal pursuits and sentiments.

In 1989, based on his theoretical and practical achievements in the fields of architecture and urban planning in the past decades, Wu published a monograph called "A General Theory of Architecture", explicating his thoughts on architecture from the perspectives of settlement, region, culture, science and technology, policy and law, professionalism, education, art, methodology, as well as his proposals to structure the general theory of architecture. As the first systematic theoretical work on modern architecture in the country, this book demonstrates his rational ideas on the academic scope and innovative concepts of architecture. It deals with the fundamental issues of nature, and the importance and the scientific base of architecture as a discipline from a broader and higher perspective. In this book, he sets up, on the basis of his persistent studies on historic experiences and relative theories and in accordance with the specific situations of China, a systematic framework of architectural theory. He puts forward some constructive suggestions to deal with the practical issues concerning architectural design and urban planning. He also advocates that architects should always keep in mind social responsibilities and professional ethics. This book can be regarded as an outcome of his long-lasting efforts under the influence of LIANG Si'cheng, LIN Huiyin, and Eliel Saarinen to search for a possible way for the development of Chinese architecture with reference to both Chinese and Western cultures, traditional architecture and modern culture. Since the publication, the book has attracted attention in the field of architecture in China and is considered "a necessary textbook for architects". In 1991, the book was awarded the First Prize for Advances of Science & Technology by the Education Committee of China.

In 1999, the 20th Congress of UIA took place in Beijing and the Beijing Charter drafted by Wu for this Congress was unanimously approved by the General Council. This event symbolizes his thoughts about the General Theory of Architecture and the Sciences of Human Settlements, which are accepted by architects overseas. More importantly, it changes the dominant role of western architectural theories in the international field of architecture. As an interpretation of the Beijing Charter, Wu published at the same time a monograph titled "Future of Architecture: Contemplating at the Turn of the New Millennium". He put forward some new rational ideas about architecture at the crucial period of its development, forming a strong contrast of two theoretical trends emerging in the international architecture competitions in recent years, which is anti-formalism advocating disorders and formalism upholding authorities.

B.4 New Thoughts on the New Master Plan of Beijing

"One cannot make a plan for a local site if he does not have a thought about the whole, while one cannot make a plan for a short period if he does not have a thought about the long term." This is an exact depiction of the great efforts that Wu has made for the rational urban development of Beijing in recent years.

Wu started his research on the urban development of Greater Beijing Region in the mid-1980s. Since the mid-1990s, when Beijing stepped into a period of accelerating urban development, he has put forward a series of constructive suggestions to the Beijing Municipal Government from the perspective of urban planning. Entrusted by Beijing Municipal Government in 2002, he presided over the research on the spatial development strategies of Beijing. Some of the outcomes of this research, such as the suggestions to reinforce the radiating influence of "two axes", that is the traditional central axis from north to south and the modern axis, Chang'an Avenue, from east to west; to encourage the growth of "two corridors", that is the development corridor in the east and the ecological corridor in the west; and to restructure the urban development of Beijing into a multi-centered pattern composed of the urban centers and suburban centers in the urban areas, as well as the new cities in the suburban areas, have been adopted by the new Master Plan of Beijing. The Plan was officially approved by the Central Government at the beginning of 2005.

Real city planning must relate to regional planning. It would be impossible to precisely define the functional role and the spatial organization of a city if the strategies for its development could not be dealt with from a wider regional perspective. As one of the three mega-city regions of China, the Greater Beijing Region suffers considerably from the deficiency of research and practice of regional planning when compared to the Yangtze River Delta Region and Pearl River Delta Region. The current state of urban development in Greater Beijing Region is far from satisfaction. On the one hand, the lack of coordination between Beijing and Tianjin in industrial development has resulted in the duplication of industrial structure of the two metropolises. This has, to some extent, affected the economic growth of Tianjin. On the other hand, the lack of regional coordination in urban development leads to the widening of regional disparities, particularly a strong contrast between the flourishing urban areas and the backward rural areas. Regarding Beijing, the dominant metropolis of Greater Beijing Region, its urban development has been concentrated to the limited built-up areas for a long time. The continuous expansion of the built-up areas brings about urban sprawl in the suburban areas and the large-scale destruction of the Old City of Beijing. Today, most of the employment is concentrated in the central area while most of the residences are scattered on the suburban areas. Beijing has to face the huge problems of traffic congestion and environment deterioration.

"In order to solve the problems of urban development of Beijing, we shall firstly review Beijing's urban development from a broader regional perspective. In other words, the problems of urban development of Beijing can only be solved when the development strategies of the Greater Beijing Region have been formulated." This was once Wu's appeal and it is a reality today.

Wu points out that the construction cause of China calls for a great number of professional talents and he always feels obliged to make use of his rich experiences and knowledge to guide the young generations.

Though already in his 80s, Wu is still working hard on research on regional planning, sciences of human settlements, regeneration of old cities, and so on, hoping to make more contributions to urban planning and development in China.

图书在版编目（CIP）数据

吴良镛论人居环境科学=WU Liangyong: Essays on the Sciences of Human Settlements in China / 吴良镛著. --北京：清华大学出版社，2010.9

ISBN 978-7-302-23837-9

Ⅰ.①吴…　Ⅱ.①吴…　Ⅲ.①居住环境—环境科学—研究—中国　Ⅳ.①X21

中国版本图书馆CIP数据核字（2010）第176460号

责任编辑：徐晓飞
责任校对：王淑云
责任印制：孟凡玉
出版发行：清华大学出版社　　　　　　　　　地　　　址：北京清华大学学研大厦 A 座
　　　　　http://www.tup.com.cn　　　　　　　邮　　　编：100084
　　　社　　总　　机：010-62770175　　　　邮　　　购：010-62786544
　　　投稿与读者服务：010-62776969，c-service@tup.tsinghua.edu.cn
　　　质　量　反　馈：010-62772015，zhiliang@tup.tsinghua.edu.cn
印　装　者：北京嘉实印刷有限公司
经　　销：全国新华书店
开　　本：185×260　印　张：9　字　数：157 千字
版　　次：2010 年 9 月第 1 版　　　印　　次：2010 年 9 月第1次印刷
印　　数：1～2000
定　　价：45.00 元

产品编号：033512-01